Bad Blood at Harlow's Bend

Scott Connor

A Black Horse Western

ROBERT HALE

© Scott Connor 2019
First published in Great Britain 2019

ISBN 978-0-7198-2932-1

The Crowood Press
The Stable Block
Crowood Lane
Ramsbury
Marlborough
Wiltshire SN8 2HR

www.bhwesterns.com

Robert Hale is an imprint
of The Crowood Press

Typeset by
Derek Doyle & Associates, Shaw Heath
Printed and bound in Great Britain by
4Bind Ltd, Stevenage, SG1 2XT

PROLOGUE

Sheriff Finlay O'Toole shoved Lorimer Hall into Clear Creek's law office and bundled him along until he stood beside his desk.

'You're in serious trouble, son,' he said and then took a long look at the cell in the corner of the room.

Lorimer gulped, but when Finlay settled down behind his desk, he breathed a sigh of relief and sat on the chair facing him.

'I didn't do nothing,' he said with his eyes downcast. 'I was just standing outside my pa's forge when the shooting started. Then I was so scared I ran for my life.'

Lorimer looked up and gave a hopeful smile, but Finlay was glaring at him.

'That's an interesting story. The trouble is I don't believe it. Tell me another one.'

'It's the only one I've got. I—'

'Enough!' Finlay snapped. He slammed a fist on the desk emphasizing his demand. 'I'll tell you what I reckon happened. Two men asked you to do them a favour. You're a young man who wants respect. You rarely get it, but these men treated you as an equal, so you went along with what they asked, except you didn't know they wanted to raid the poker game.'

Lorimer shook his head and gulped, but he failed to moisten his dry mouth.

'I don't know what you're talking about.'

'You might not, but I reckon Budd Ewing will.' Finlay smiled when the revelation that he knew Lorimer had got his friend involved made the young man wince. 'He's sensible. He'll tell me everything.'

'I don't know what Budd did.'

'You sure don't know plenty,' Finlay chuckled. 'That's not important. I just need the names of the men who told you to stand outside the forge and look out for trouble.'

Lorimer stared at Finlay, hoping his firm gaze would make him look innocent and hide the fact that he regretted letting the Devlin brothers persuade him to help them with their escapade. He met Finlay's eyes for several seconds before he had to look aside.

'I don't know what you mean.'

'Your father will be disappointed. When he finds

out his only son has rebelled against him the shock will probably kill him.'

Lorimer's heart thudded with the terrible thought that Finlay was right, and no matter how severe the punishment the sheriff might mete out, it would be less troubling than how his pa would react. He gnawed at his bottom lip, as if that might help him to avoid blurting out the information Finlay wanted.

'I can't help you,' he said, his voice emerging as a croak.

Finlay leaned forward and placed his elbows on the desk, his confident smile showing he knew he was close to breaking his prisoner.

'You have to. Your father is distraught, Carl Templeman is nowhere to be found, Benedict Harlow got wounded and Manford Wigfall could die. If he does, no matter that your involvement was minor, you'll spend a long time in jail.'

'How long?'

'You'll get ten years. For a fresh-faced young man like you that could be a lifetime, but it doesn't have to be that way. If you help me, it'll prove you were an unwitting part of what happened today and you can go back home to Harlow's Bend.'

Lorimer looked at the cell in the corner and imagined spending ten years in a confined space with hundreds of other men, all as rough and as violent as the Devlins. Then he turned back to the sheriff.

'I never thought anyone would get hurt.'

'I know that, so what's it to be, son?' Finlay smiled. 'Are you going to continue claiming you don't know nothing and go to jail, or are you going to talk and have a good life?'

CHAPTER 1

Ten years later. . . .

Lorimer Hall drew his horse to a halt. The town of Clear Creek was beyond the next hill and despite his resolution to return to his hometown he now wondered whether it would be worth the trouble.

If things were the same as they had been when he'd left, several people would probably try to run him out of town and the rest wouldn't welcome seeing him again. So to help him judge how bad a reception he might get he headed towards the house of the man who would probably be least pleased to see him, Manford Wigfall.

He didn't know if Manford would still be living there, but when he approached the house he was outside and getting ready to leave. Lorimer drew up beside the gate, around twenty yards from the house.

'Am I welcome?' he called.

Manford turned away from his horse and then winced, presumably after recognizing him. He mounted up and rode towards him.

'I never expected to see you around these parts again,' he said as he stopped in the gateway. 'Now that I have, I don't want to do it again.'

With that Manford moved on. As he passed by he pressed a hand to his side, presumably as a reminder of where he'd been shot ten years ago.

Manford then rode off towards town. As his reaction had been better than Lorimer had feared, he rode after him at a slower pace.

Manford drew ahead until he was a quarter-mile away, but when he reached the side of the hill he stopped. He glanced back at Lorimer before looking ahead.

Then, with a whip of the reins, he turned his horse and galloped towards a derelict house at the base of the hill. A few moments later Lorimer saw a possible reason for his behaviour when two men came running around the side of the hill.

They were halfway up the slope and when they stopped they levelled guns on the fleeing rider. Two crisp gunshots rang out, but Manford was already a hundred yards away.

The men faced each other and conducted a brief debate before retreating back around the side of the hill. Lorimer didn't know the reason for this altercation, but without thinking he hurried his horse on towards the house.

He kept one eye on the hill and the other on the fleeing Manford. The men didn't reappear, while Manford stopped beside the house and peered around anxiously until he faced Lorimer.

Lorimer slowed down so Manford wouldn't view his action as threatening and shook his head to convey he wasn't involved in the attempted ambush.

His behaviour appeared to placate Manford as he dismounted and hurried to the side wall. He drew his six-shooter and hunkered down in a position where he could watch the part of the slope where the men had fired at him.

'What's this about?' Lorimer called when he was thirty yards from the house.

Manford cast him a surly glare, but he didn't reply. As he also didn't object to his presence, Lorimer carried on and dismounted.

He stood in a position where he could watch the parts of the hill that Manford wouldn't be able to see. For several minutes he considered the scene before Manford looked at him.

'We're a peaceful town,' he said. 'We've had one shooting in the last year. Then you come back.'

Manford gestured angrily at him, but Lorimer only shook his head.

'This hasn't got nothing to do with me,' he said.

Lorimer raised an eyebrow, inviting Manford to offer an alternative explanation. Manford sighed and then shrugged, seeming to accept he might have been hasty in blaming him.

'I guess it's well known I head into town for the monthly poker game. Maybe someone heard I'd have money on me.' Manford snorted a laugh. 'After all, I usually don't have any after the game.'

Lorimer laughed. 'After what happened ten years ago I'm surprised you still play.'

'It's a good tradition, except the players have changed.' Manford frowned, presumably acknowledging that one of the former players was Lorimer's father. 'We meet in Ewing's saloon.'

'Is that Budd Ewing's place?'

Manford nodded. 'Your old partner in crime changed after you left town. He turned out fine and started a thriving business.'

Manford raised his hat to run fingers through his hair, the nervous action suggesting that his declaration had troubled him. With his bout of good humour ending, he turned to the hill and looked out for the gunmen.

Several minutes passed in silence. As it was unclear how long the impasse would continue, or even if the men were still nearby, Lorimer moved away from Manford.

More of the hill became visible and he saw neither the gunmen nor any terrain that could be providing them with cover. With the feeling growing that they had, in fact, moved on, Lorimer raised a hand to get Manford's attention, but then he saw movement.

The gunmen had doubled back and headed around the hill. Now they were riding towards the other side of the house.

'Behind you!' he called.

Manford took several moments to register Lorimer's warning. Then, with a flinch, he glanced over his shoulder, but he was too close to the wall to see the men.

Lorimer gestured indicating the area where the riders were before he broke into a run back towards Manford. He sprinted with his head down until the house blocked his view of the riders, after which he straightened up.

Manford scurried along beside the wall and when he reached the corner he nodded to Lorimer as hoofbeats could now be heard. He glanced along the back of the house, but then shrugged and moved beyond the corner, presumably because he had failed to see anyone.

Taking one steady pace at a time he edged sideways. Then he must have caught sight of the gunmen as he twisted round and made to run back to safety.

A gunshot rang out, kicking dirt at his heels. He sped up, but a second shot blasted making him cry out and clutch a hand to his bloodied side before he toppled over.

As Manford ploughed face first into the dirt, Lorimer winced and carried on to the house where he pressed his back to the side wall. He peered at Manford, but when the downed man remained still, Lorimer moved back to the corner.

He looked along the front of the house. The gunmen were twenty yards away and they had already levelled guns on the corner.

They both fired, forcing Lorimer to jerk back out of sight. He pressed his back to the wall as he considered his next move and then decided to use his opponents' tactic and try to be in the place they would least expect him to be.

He hurried along the side wall and turned down the back of the house. When he reached a window he stopped and glanced inside.

The interior of the house was a shell, letting him see through the windows at the front. The gunmen weren't visible, so he clambered up on to the sill.

As he was swinging his legs down on the other side, hoofbeats pounded nearby. He froze and listened, fearing that his opponents were getting reinforcements, but after a few moments he noted that the sounds were getting further away.

He swung back down outside and moved on. Sure enough, when the riders came into view they were galloping away.

In irritation Lorimer loosed off a shot at their fleeing forms, but that made both men return fire.

14

He retreated into cover at the back of the house and when he next checked on them the men were riding out of sight around the base of the hill.

With a sigh Lorimer headed back to Manford and hunkered down beside him. To his surprise he was still breathing, but only shallowly, so he rolled him over on to his back.

Manford uttered a pained groan and looked at him with half-closed eyes.

'Gone?' he murmured.

'They have, and clearly they wanted you after all,' Lorimer said.

Manford grimaced and arched his back as a spasm of pain racked his body. When his expression became calmer he exhaled deeply. Then he became still, making Lorimer reckon he'd breathed his last, but after a few moments he dragged in another tortured breath.

'Tell me one thing,' Manford gasped. 'Did you turn out fine?'

Lorimer smiled. 'You knew me when I was young and I made a bad mistake back then, but since I left Clear Creek I've been a good man and led a decent life.'

Manford breathed a sigh of relief. 'I'm pleased to hear that, and I'm sorry about your father. He was an honourable man and he sure suffered from. . . .'

Manford trailed off and looked at the sky. He murmured something, but Lorimer couldn't hear what he said. Then his eyes became glassy.

Presently, Lorimer accepted that Manford had died, although he watched him for several more minutes before nudging his shoulder. When that failed to get a reaction he looked the body over.

He noted a bulge in Manford's jacket pocket. He investigated and located a billfold that contained over fifty dollars.

A search of the other pockets revealed a silver watch. It had an ornate inscription on the back and looked shiny and valuable.

Lorimer hefted the money and watch on his palm. Then he pocketed them and headed to his horse.

CHAPTER 2

Lorimer led Manford's horse, with Manford's body draped over the back, as he set off for Clear Creek.

He embarked on a roundabout journey that gave the hill a wide berth. This route ensured that he didn't come across the gunmen again and the incident stopped him worrying about how his homecoming would go, so he was in relatively good spirits when he rode into town.

The law office was opposite Ewing's saloon. He had already decided that even if he did nothing else here he would meet his old friend, but as the body was gathering an interested group of onlookers he went straight into the office.

The sheriff was already coming to the door. To Lorimer's relief he wasn't Sheriff O'Toole and neither was he someone he'd ever met before.

Lorimer provided his name and briefly reported on what had happened, and the sheriff, Oran

Roswell, told him to stay in the office and fix himself a coffee while he dealt with the body.

When Roswell returned fifteen minutes later Lorimer was already on his second mug. He gave a more detailed account, although it wasn't much use as he had been near to the gunmen for only a brief time and he hadn't seen their faces.

'I'm obliged for what you did,' Roswell said when Lorimer had finished talking. 'Helpful strangers are always welcome in Clear Creek.'

Lorimer sighed. He had hoped to avoid mentioning his personal situation, but he reckoned he couldn't avoid it now.

'I'm not a stranger,' he said. 'I haven't been here for some years, but I'm. . . . I'm a relative of Jeremiah Hall. I came to pay my respects.'

Roswell gave a sympathetic smile. 'Then I'm sorry. We were all saddened to see him go last year.'

'Last year?' Lorimer tipped back his hat and rubbed his brow in surprise. 'I met someone a few weeks ago who told me what had happened. I'd thought he'd died only. . . .'

Lorimer trailed off as he accepted he'd made a mistake. The messenger had only passed on gossip and he had just assumed his father had died recently.

'He was buried at Harlow's Bend. It's what he wanted.'

Lorimer nodded and, with Roswell then heading

to the door with the intention of visiting the scene of the gunfight, he left the office. He stood at the hitching rail and watched Roswell ride out of town before turning to the saloon.

He was now unsure whether he wanted to talk with Budd next or head to Harlow's Bend, so he stood for several minutes until he noticed a woman walking down his side of the main drag. She was clad in black and had her head down so her bonnet hid most of her face, but he was sure she was Christina White.

She was the first person he'd seen in town that he recognized, but he didn't want to meet her again. When he'd been younger Budd had been sweet on her, but he had left town before he'd found out how that worked out.

She was clutching a basket to her chest and she appeared to be deep in thought. As she showed no sign of having noticed him, before she reached him Lorimer set off across the main drag.

He walked into the saloon and found that Budd's older brother Wheeler was serving behind the bar. Wheeler watched him approach with his eyes narrowed and then gave a small smile of recognition.

'Howdy, Wheeler, it's been a while,' Lorimer said. He looked around when Wheeler acknowledged him with a disinterested nod. 'Is Budd here?'

'Budd's dead,' Wheeler said. 'He got shot up two months ago.'

'He's been killed?' Lorimer blew out his cheeks and sat on a barstool. 'I was told this is a peaceful town these days and there's been only one shooting in the last year.' Lorimer snorted a rueful laugh, as the person who had told him that had then been shot, but Wheeler looked at him levelly and gave no sign that this information had reached him.

'That's right, and Budd was the man who got shot.'

'I'm sorry to hear that. What happened?'

Wheeler leaned on the bar facing Lorimer. 'He got into an argument with Glenn Harlow at Harlow's Bend. Glenn gunned him down.'

Lorimer nodded. Glenn was another name he remembered from his earlier life here. Glenn was married to Christina White's older sister, Abigail, and his father Benedict was the other man who had been shot during the Devlin brothers' raid on the poker game.

'I remember that after Benedict got hurt Glenn and Budd often argued.'

'They did, and one day that feud got out of hand.' Wheeler gestured outside indicating the edge of town. 'Glenn's in the jailhouse waiting to spend the rest of his life in Brookville jail. He'll have to go soon or Clear Creek might get its first lynching, and I'll be there to support it.'

A customer murmured his support for Wheeler's declaration, and with Wheeler glowering angrily,

Lorimer decided he'd heard enough. He thanked him for the information and again offered his condolences before heading outside.

As he wouldn't be able to renew his friendship with Budd, he figured there was only thing left for him to do here. He returned to his horse and mounted up, and then rode out of town towards the creek.

He took the long route to Harlow's Bend that he used to enjoy that went along the meandering side of the creek. As he doubted he would ever return to Clear Creek he dallied beside the water.

He dismounted several times and watched the water drift by. It was only when he could see the other homestead that was on the bend in the creek that he figured he'd put off visiting his father's grave for long enough.

This property was where Benedict Harlow lived. Benedict's parents had been the first to settle here and when later the Halls had arrived they'd been welcomed.

Jeremiah Hall had built a forge on the far side of the bend and he and the Harlows had got on fine. Later others had settled the area further away from the creek and founded the main settlement.

While he'd been growing up Benedict had always been eager to talk, but as his son had killed Budd Ewing he didn't want to meet him.

He rode inland to give the homestead a wide

21

berth and when the far side of Harlow's Bend came into view he was surprised to see smoke rising up from his father's forge while two men were moving around in front of the house. He had figured that anyone who took over doing that line of the work would do so nearer to the town.

The men turned to him, so Lorimer raised a hand in greeting while he looked around for the grave. He presumed it would be near to his mother's grave, but he couldn't recall where that was, so he moved on to the house.

Closer to, he saw that the men were burly and they were wearing blackened aprons confirming they had taken over his father's business.

'I'm pleased the forge is still being used,' he called when he drew up.

'We do good work these days,' one man said. He introduced himself as Vester with his colleague being his brother Moody. 'What do you want?'

'Where was Jeremiah Hall buried?'

The men peered at him and then turned to each other, their furrowed brows suggesting they might have worked out who he was. Moody then went into the house while Vester folded his arms and glared at him.

Lorimer could see no reason for them to delay giving him an answer, but presently Moody returned with the woman he'd seen earlier, Christina. She looked at Lorimer with a weary air.

'I saw you in town,' she said. 'I had a feeling you'd come here.'

'That shouldn't be surprising,' Lorimer said. 'This was once my home and my father's buried here somewhere.'

Christina sneered. 'Why should you care about either of those things? You've not been here in ten years and it's your fault he's in the ground.'

'I have my reasons for not viewing Harlow's Bend as my home no more, but how can his death be my fault when I've not even been here to—'

'Because having a son like you made him turn to drink. In the end the liquor was all he cared about.'

Lorimer sighed. 'I'm sorry to hear that, but I'm pleased someone is living here and I just want to see where he is. Then I'll leave you to your business.'

'Just go.' She gestured at Moody and Vester. 'My cousins are protective of me and despite what I feel about you I wouldn't want you to get hurt.'

The two men flanked her and folded their arms in a show of truculence. Lorimer rubbed his jaw as he wondered how he could plead his case, but then he noticed something he perhaps ought to have considered before and which provided a possible reason for her unhelpfulness.

He dismounted, walked a few paces closer to her, and removed his hat.

'I'm sorry for your recent loss, assuming that's why you're wearing black,' he said with a low tone.

'Was it Budd Ewing?'

'It was,' she said.

'As you know, Budd was my friend. I only found out a few hours ago that he'd been killed.'

'And I hope you're feeling some of the pain I've felt. He was a good man and the only problems he faced stemmed from what you made him do ten years ago, so I'm thankful you left as you'd have ruined his life.'

'I'm thankful for that, too. It's good to hear he had a better life than I've had.'

He backed away for a pace and gave a thin smile. He hoped that now she'd explained the reason for her anger she might tell him where his father was buried, but instead she glanced at Vester and Moody and then turned away.

Her silent instruction made Vester take a step towards him while Moody headed to the forge and picked up an axe handle that was propped up against the wall.

'I'll leave,' Lorimer said as Moody turned to him and swung the handle from side to side.

'You are,' Vester said with a grin.

With quick steps Vester walked up to him. Lorimer turned away to mount his horse, but he wasn't quick enough as Vester slapped a hand on his shoulder and hurled him away.

Lorimer crashed to the ground and went tumbling. When he stopped rolling he found that he'd moved towards Moody, who loomed up over him with the handle raised above his head.

In desperation Lorimer rolled to the side as the cudgel came crashing down and buried itself in the ground where his chest had been a few moments earlier. Lorimer rolled twice more and then got up on one knee facing Moody, who advanced on him while swinging the handle.

Lorimer set his weight forward and, when Moody was two paces from him and the handle was moving away from him, he kicked off from the ground. On the run he slammed into Moody's hips and wrapped his arms around him, but he managed to shove his opponent backwards for only two paces.

Moody slapped the cudgel down over Lorimer's back, making him drop to his knees before he bundled him away with a swing of his right leg. Lorimer moved to get up, but he had yet to gain his feet when Vester advanced on him from behind and grabbed his shoulder with one hand and the seat of his pants with the other.

Vester then tossed him aside and again Lorimer went rolling away. When he came to rest on his back he was winded and disorientated, but he forced himself to stand up.

He scrambled away from his opponents, but to his relief they hadn't advanced on him. While they'd been tussling Christina had returned to the house, so with as much dignity as he could muster he batted the dust from his pants and jacket and faced them.

'That was a warning,' Moody said. 'At a time like this our cousin doesn't need to be bothered by the likes of you, so don't ever come back to Harlow's Bend again.'

Both men glared at him, but then Vester looked away towards the creek before again fixing him with his gaze. Lorimer glanced that way and noted that Vester had looked at a line of trees.

Now that he'd seen the trees he recalled that this was where his mother had been buried, and his father would often sit there to watch the water drift by.

Lorimer nodded to them and then turned to his horse. They made no further aggressive moves, so in short order he mounted up and rode away from the house.

Fifty yards on he glanced back. Vester was walking to the forge while Moody continued to watch him, but Lorimer still stopped and turned to the creek.

From this position he could see two mounds beyond the trees.

'Goodbye, Pa,' he murmured under his breath and lowered his head for a moment.

Then, figuring he'd done everything he had intended to do here, he rode away.

CHAPTER 3

When Lorimer left Harlow's Bend he was surprised to see that the sun was already approaching the horizon. He hadn't intended to return to town, but he figured he must have spent longer beside the creek than he'd thought he had.

As he didn't welcome the thought of sleeping under the stars that night he rode back into Clear Creek. Ewing's saloon had a room available as well as providing food, so he availed himself of both.

He wasn't interested in learning any more about events in town over the last ten years, so he didn't encourage Wheeler to talk and neither did he volunteer any information. After eating he left the saloon to check on his horse, but while he was in the stable Sheriff Roswell sought him out.

'Are you having any luck catching Manford Wigfall's killers?' Lorimer asked.

'They covered their tracks and I've found no

trace of them,' Roswell said. 'Worse, you're the only one who's seen them, so I don't have any clues about who they are or where they went.'

'Then is there anything else I can do to help you?'

'I don't reckon you can help me with that problem, but you can help me with another one. I need someone to escort Glenn Harlow to Brookville jail.'

Lorimer turned away from his horse and raised an eyebrow in surprise.

'Surely someone else can do it.'

Roswell uttered a long sigh. 'To be honest, you're the least worst option I've considered. Feelings are running high and I don't know who I can trust to make sure he doesn't get lynched, but you've not been involved in what's been going on here recently. Even better, you went to Manford's aid and you're related to Jeremiah Hall, so I reckon you're a fair and reliable man.'

Lorimer shook his head. 'I'm not sure about that, but I'm leaving town tomorrow and I won't be coming back.'

Roswell smiled. 'That's ideal. Once you've got him to jail I have no further use for you.'

Lorimer lowered his head as he sought a better excuse. He didn't want to spend time with Budd's killer and he figured that explaining he was Jeremiah's son would probably make the sheriff desist, as it would show he knew Budd as well as Glenn.

On the other hand Roswell was clearly desperate for help and the money he'd taken off Manford's body was the only funds he had.

'How much?'

'I'll pay you a hundred dollars.'

This was more than he'd expected, so Lorimer nodded. He then accompanied the sheriff to the law office where he received his instructions and, in a show of good faith, his payment.

He returned to the saloon where he went straight to his room. Despite the troubling events of the day he quickly got to sleep.

In the morning he rose before first light and headed to the jailhouse. Sheriff Roswell wasn't there, so a warden brought Glenn from his cell.

As the prisoner shuffled towards him with his shoulders hunched over, Lorimer tensed up to avoid showing any emotion, but as it turned out he felt only a vague sense of unease. Glenn didn't show any sign that he recognized him, removing the possibility that Lorimer wouldn't be allowed to take custody of him.

The warden bound Glenn's hands before him. Then Lorimer led him out the back of the jailhouse.

Glenn mounted the waiting horse and Lorimer was given rope to keep a secure hold of the prisoner. When the warden returned to the jailhouse he followed the sheriff's instructions and rode to the north with the prisoner in tow, ensuring they reached the cover of a small wood quickly.

Whenever he looked at Glenn he was glancing around nervously as if he shared Roswell's fear that someone would attack them, but on the way they saw nobody. Then they moved on to the creek and headed downriver, skirting the northern edge of the water.

By the time the sun rose they were a dozen miles from town and they'd moved past the sprinkling of homesteads that surrounded Clear Creek.

Lorimer reckoned this was a good time to take a break and define terms with his charge. He dismounted and tugged Glenn's rope, encouraging him to join him on the ground.

'It'll take us until late tomorrow to reach Brookville,' he said. 'I hope you won't give me no trouble.'

'I won't,' Glenn mumbled with his head lowered.

Lorimer moved closer to Glenn and looked him over. The prisoner didn't meet his eye and Lorimer reckoned he really was in a morose state and he wasn't just trying to appear docile in the hope of lulling him into a false sense of security.

He still saw no reason not to browbeat him some more.

'That's sensible talking. Many people want to lynch you. I'm not like them.' Lorimer waited until

Glenn looked up and then scowled. 'I'm worse. Budd Ewing was my friend and I'd welcome you trying something just so I've got an excuse to pound you into the ground.'

Glenn narrowed his eyes. 'I remember you now. You're Lorimer Hall. You helped Budd raid that poker game all those years ago.'

'I sure did, and that should tell you everything you need to know about me.' Lorimer glared at Glenn until he gulped, and then pointed to Glenn's horse. 'Now mount up and stay quiet.'

Glenn did as he'd been asked and when they set off he rode beside him with his head down. They'd covered another mile when Glenn edged his horse in closer to him.

'I didn't kill Budd,' he said before swinging away to resume riding at the same distance from him as before.

Lorimer had suspected that Glenn would make such a claim as he laid the groundwork for a plea to be released, so he had no trouble ignoring the invitation to talk with him.

Sheriff Roswell had detailed several alternative routes he could take and Lorimer had opted to head to a flag station at Webster's Crossing. A train was due in late afternoon and Lorimer ensured they would get there in good time by maintaining a brisk pace with only one further stop at noon.

Webster's Crossing turned out to be a sprawl of

buildings set on either side of the tracks, and as they looked as if they'd been abandoned Lorimer rode to the station house. He settled Glenn down on a bench facing the tracks and then sat at the far end of the bench with the rope that secured his prisoner at the wrists played out on the platform between them.

Two hours passed quietly and Lorimer was glancing down the tracks in anticipation of seeing the train when Glenn looked at him for the first time in a while. Glenn raised an eyebrow, making Lorimer smile.

'Save your breath,' Lorimer said. 'I've heard all the excuses before.'

'I'm sure you've met plenty of criminals, but I'm not one of them,' Glenn said. He shuffled closer to Lorimer. 'As Budd's friend, you must want to know the truth about what happened to him.'

'A court worked it out. That's good enough for me.'

Glenn raised a finger and smiled, as if he'd hoped Lorimer would make that point. Lorimer groaned as he accepted he'd done what he'd wanted to avoid and engaged the prisoner in debate.

'My trial concentrated on the bad blood between me and Budd. I blamed him for getting my father shot, and when he married my wife's sister and settled nearby that made things worse. So his death looked bad for me, but it doesn't change the fact I didn't kill him.'

Lorimer frowned and looked away as he thought this through before turning back to Glenn.

'As you've told me your story, we've got no reason to speak about it again.'

'We haven't, but Budd didn't get justice. I hope his friend will do something about that.'

After escorting Glenn to jail, Lorimer intended to ride away and never think about Clear Creek again, but he also wanted the rest of the journey to be trouble free. He gave a thin smile.

'I'll see what I can find out,' he said.

Glenn murmured a sigh of relief. 'That's all I ask.'

Lorimer's guts rumbled with a twinge of remorse after giving Glenn false hope, but he dismissed the matter when he saw movement along the tracks. He narrowed his eyes and decided it didn't come from an approaching train, and after a short while he discerned two riders.

When Glenn saw where he was looking he turned towards the newcomers. Then he muttered under his breath and swirled back to face Lorimer, who also muttered to himself when he recognized the men.

'So Vester and Moody White have followed us,' he said.

'They sure have,' Glenn said with a worried gulp.

Lorimer slapped his holster. 'Don't worry. I've met them before and this time they won't get the better of me.'

CHAPTER 4

'What are you doing this far from Clear Creek?' Lorimer called when the two riders drew up at the end of the platform.

'We want to talk to Glenn,' Moody said.

'Then you've wasted a journey,' Lorimer said. 'He's not talkative.'

The brothers glanced at each other and nodded. Then Vester dismounted and walked to the middle of the platform.

He set his feet wide apart and faced the tracks. As Lorimer figured that ignoring him wouldn't make the brothers go away, he bade Glenn to stay on the bench. Then, while still holding on to the rope that secured his prisoner, he joined Vester.

'Our cousin needs answers,' Vester said. 'This is her last chance to get them.'

Lorimer shook his head. 'The trial was the last chance. Glenn must have said everything he ever

35

would back then.'

'Except he didn't say nothing anyone believed. I reckon he might be more amenable now his fate has been sealed.'

Lorimer shrugged. 'I asked him what happened to my old friend Budd. He had nothing to say about the incident.'

Vester smiled. 'Then you weren't persuasive enough, but we're not like you, as we proved back at Harlow's Bend.'

Lorimer moved a pace away from Vester.

'And I'm nothing like you, but that doesn't matter as I've heard enough. Keep away from my prisoner.'

He turned to head back to the station house, but Vester stepped to the side and raised an arm, blocking his way.

'Christina told us about you. Ten years ago you kept lookout for two outlaws while they raided a poker game, and your father was playing in that game. And you persuaded your best friend to help. So I didn't expect you'd be this dutiful.'

'When I make a promise to do something, I always see it through.'

Vester chuckled. 'How much is Sheriff Roswell paying you?'

'A hundred dollars.'

'I guess that's enough to make a man like you stand in our way. We'll pay you twenty-five dollars for fifteen minutes alone with him.'

'I reckon you two can inflict a lot of damage in that time.' Lorimer glanced at Glenn and then lowered his voice. 'Make it five minutes for fifty dollars and we have a deal.'

Vester licked his lips. 'Moody and me could inflict a lot of damage in five minutes, but that's not why we're here. We just want to ask him a few questions.'

'Then it should only take you five minutes to ask them.'

Vester rubbed his jaw as he considered the matter and then leaned towards him.

'Twenty-five now and twenty-five if we get what we want.'

Lorimer looked Vester in the eye and when he met his gaze he held out a hand. With a smile Vester withdrew the money from his pocket and slapped it on to his palm.

'Five minutes and no bruises,' Lorimer said.

When Vester grunted that he agreed to his terms Lorimer closed his hand around the money and gave the rope to him. He walked back to Glenn, who eyed him with horror.

'What have you done?' Glenn murmured.

'Don't be concerned,' Lorimer said. 'They just want to talk to you. Be honest and there'll be no trouble, but I'll be outside. If they threaten you, call out and I'll be there before they can lay a finger on you.'

Glenn looked him over with contempt, but he didn't say anything and turned to Vester and Moody. Lorimer waited until they joined them.

With a mocking show of being polite, Moody held the station house door open for Glenn and invited him to enter with a wide smile. Vester shot his brother an irritated glance as he tugged on Glenn's rope, and Glenn resisted for long enough to sneer at Lorimer. Then he headed inside.

Lorimer consulted the watch he'd stolen from Manford's body to remind Vester of the deadline. When Vester nodded he walked around the building to the other side.

There were no windows at the front, but a door was ajar. He stood beside the door and heard Moody talking, although his voice was too low for him to work out what he was saying.

As the brothers appeared to be keeping their promise to only talk with Glenn, Lorimer idled away a few minutes by sauntering towards the nearest building. He confirmed that it and the other nearby buildings weren't in use and then sauntered back.

A glance at the watch showed that most of the allotted five minutes had passed. So he leaned back against the wall and counted down from fifty.

He was about to deem he'd given the brothers enough time when Vester came around the side of the station house.

'You were right,' Vester said. 'He's not saying nothing.'

'Then I'm sorry you'll have to disappoint Christina,' Lorimer said.

'She'll be pleased we tried.' Vester frowned. 'She's not usually unfriendly like she was yesterday, but she's had a lot to deal with recently, what with her husband's death making the rift with our other cousin even worse, so we don't like anyone upsetting her.'

'I can understand that. Living near to kin you're feuding with must make it hard for you all.' Lorimer sighed. 'And I'm obliged you showed me where my father had been buried.'

Vester looked at him oddly as if he couldn't recall his small act of kindness, but he dismissed the matter with a shrug.

'You might have heard bad tales about Jeremiah's final years, but he had some good times, too.'

'I'm relieved to hear that.'

Vester leaned closer to him. 'Budd treated him as if he was his own father. When he married, Glenn and his wife were living with Benedict, so Jeremiah let Budd and Christina live with him until Budd could get the saloon he'd just bought fixed up, except they liked being there so much they stayed.'

Lorimer smiled as he thought back to his time living on Harlow's Bend.

'It's a good place. I have fond memories of

fishing down by the creek with my father.'

'I've done that a few times myself.' Vester tipped back his hat and breathed deeply, as if he was enjoying the invigorating air by the water. 'When Jeremiah needed help with his work, Christina suggested he employ us two. That worked out, so we're still there carrying on his good work.'

'That's fine. I never had no desire to get roasted and burnt every day.'

Vester frowned. 'So what was so bad about your childhood? You had a good father and good friends, except sometimes you make it sound like hell.'

'I guess it was fine, up until the day me and Budd made a big mistake.' Lorimer wondered whether he wanted to explain further, but he reckoned Vester might be keeping him talking so Moody could have more time with Glenn. He pushed away from the wall and moved to step around Vester. 'But that doesn't matter no more.'

Vester watched him walk by, but he made no move to leave.

'It doesn't, but I'd like to know the truth,' he called after Lorimer, making him stop. 'Budd never wanted to talk about what happened that day.'

Lorimer shook his head, now sure that Vester was just delaying him.

'You sure are interested in the truth today,' he said as he set off.

Vester hurried after him as Lorimer walked round to the back of the station house. When Lorimer looked through the door, to his irritation Moody and Glenn weren't there.

'What's wrong?' Vester asked with a light tone, as if nothing was amiss.

Lorimer swirled round to confront him, but he saw that the brothers' horses were still at the end of the platform. As the small settlement had few places where Glenn could have been taken, he didn't waste time demanding an explanation and walked away.

When he reached the corner of the building he looked for the most promising place to search first, but then he heard a creaking sound. He turned and then slapped a hand to his mouth in horror.

Moody was facing him. His arms were folded and he was smirking. Between them was Glenn and he was dangling on the end of the rope that had previously secured him.

Lorimer set off towards him, but then stopped when he saw the full extent of what had happened. Glenn had been hanged.

One end of the rope had been wrapped around his neck and the other end had been slung over a projection on the apex of the roof. Then Glenn had been hoisted up into the air.

'You sure aren't observant for a guard,' Moody said, making Vester laugh.

Lorimer noted the gag around Glenn's mouth that would have stopped him shouting for help, and he assumed the lynching had been carried out when he had walked away from the station house. Even so, he had to admit he had been lax in failing to hear what had happened.

Lorimer moved on to stand in front of the dangling body. The dull red flush suffusing Glenn's face and his blank eyes showed he would be wasting his time if he tried to cut him down quickly.

He stood there for a while, feeling too numb to even remonstrate with Glenn's assailants. With him not reacting, Vester joined Moody and the two men murmured to each other before they stood on either side of him.

'So you're still the same person you were ten years ago,' Vester said. 'Back then you were paid to stand outside a building and someone died, and it's the same again now.'

Lorimer didn't think it was worth mentioning that ten years ago he hadn't been paid and nobody had died. When he didn't reply, Moody stood in front of him.

'Don't ever speak of this to anyone,' he said. 'If you do, we'll tell everyone how co-operative you were.'

He chuckled, but when Lorimer continued to look at the body he turned on his heels and walked towards his horse. Vester then stood in front of him.

'Before I forget, here's the second half of your payment.' Vester withdrew a wad of bills from his pocket. When Lorimer made no move to claim the money he tossed it on the ground. 'As promised, Glenn doesn't have no bruises on him.'

Vester laughed. Then he joined Moody in walking away.

CHAPTER 5

Lorimer wasn't sure how long he stood looking up at Glenn's body, but he shook off his torpor when a whistle sounded.

He confirmed that the train was approaching, although it was only a small gleaming object in the distance. Vester and Moody were no longer visible.

Moving quickly, he collected his horse and mounted up. With the extra height he was able to cut down Glenn's body. Then he dragged it away from the tracks to the front of the station house.

The train was now close enough that a passenger might see him if he were to head across open ground to a building, so he laid the body down in the shadows. Then he stood with his back to the wall while listening to the train rattle closer.

As he'd expected the train passed the station without stopping, so when it had moved out of sight, he took the body into the station house and left it in a corner.

He sat on the bench outside, and with his head in his hands he tried to figure out what he should do next. He reckoned that if he told anyone what had happened – with his story amended to avoid incurring the White brothers' wrath – he would be in trouble, but when Glenn failed to arrive at the jail he would be in just as much trouble.

With both alternatives being unpalatable he sat morosely until sundown, by which time it was too late to do anything that day. He slipped into the station house and sat in the opposite corner to the body.

While the darkness deepened he stared at the corpse. Only when he could no longer see it did he try to get some sleep.

After shuffling around on the floor uneasily for several hours he dozed at last, and when he awoke weak moonlight was streaming in through the only window. He steeled himself to look in the corner and when he turned in that direction he flinched.

By a horrible coincidence the moonlight illuminated the corner where the body was lying, making it appear unnaturally prominent. Worse, Glenn's eyes were shiny and accusing.

'I never meant for that to happen,' Lorimer said. 'They lied to me.'

Lorimer turned away, annoyed with himself for having spoken, but he still felt as if Glenn's dead eyes were staring at him. He turned back and in the last few moments the moonlight had grown stronger, making the eyes look even brighter.

'Quit looking at me! You deserved that. You killed my friend.'

Lorimer got up on to his haunches and glared at the corpse, daring it to retort. It didn't, but a more troubling thought made him speak again.

'Except you didn't kill him, did you?'

He stood up and then screeched when the body closed its eyes. He raised an arm in front of his face, his heart pounding in alarm as he fought down the urge to run out of the building.

When he lowered his arm the eyes were, in fact, open. Now he saw that after changing position he had no longer been able to see the moonlight reflected in the eyes, and that had made it look as if Glenn had somehow reacted to his question.

He ducked down and confirmed his theory. Then he walked to the door and looked outside until his breathing and heart rate calmed down.

When he returned he avoided looking at the corpse and presently he dozed again. The next time he awoke the sun was up and when he glanced at the body it no longer held his attention as it had done during the night.

He headed outside and got ready to leave. He figured he should keep his options open until the last moment as to whether to take the body or leave it, so he avoided looking at the station house.

By the time he was ready to mount up he'd decided he never wanted to see the body again, so he looked for anything that might prove he'd been here. His gaze alighted on the side of the building and he realized he hadn't claimed the money Vester had given him the previous day.

He moved on and located the bills lying beside the wall. He knelt and reached for the money only to flinch away when a shadow flittered across the wall.

He twisted round while falling backwards so he ended up sitting and leaning back against the wall with his gun drawn. Nobody was there, although a hawk was gliding by.

With a hand raised to shield his eyes from the sun, he watched the bird and then glanced at the apex of the roof where Glenn had been hanged.

'You sure are twitchy today,' he murmured to himself and then moved to holster his gun, but he failed to touch leather and the gun clattered to the ground.

His clumsiness made him mutter under his breath and on the second attempt he slipped the gun away. Then he reached for the money, but to his horror the hand shook, so he drew it back.

He sat there for a while wondering whether he wanted the money. With his thoughts dwelling on his financial situation he withdrew the stolen watch from his pocket.

Now that he thought about it, this could have been one of the valuables the Devlin brothers had wanted to steal ten years ago, but it no longer looked as shiny and as valuable as it had done when he'd taken it. He moved to hurl it away, but then stopped the movement with his arm thrust out.

He chided himself for considering such an action and pocketed the watch and money, this time without mishap. Then he headed back into the station house and stood over the corpse.

'As I'm not thinking straight today, I guess we have a story to tell,' he said. 'I hope it'll be a good one.'

Lorimer doubted it would be, but he still took hold of the body and dragged it outside. Ten minutes later he was heading back to Clear Creek with Glenn's horse laden down with the body trailing behind him.

It had taken him most of the previous day to reach the station, but this time he travelled at a slower pace, so it was after sundown when he rode into town. This was fine with him as fewer people would probably see him and his cargo, but the longer ride hadn't let him work out what would be sensible to tell Sheriff Roswell.

It was only when he went into the law office that he decided to act as he had done the first time he'd gone in there ten years ago and say as little as he could get away with.

'I'm returning your hundred dollars,' he said and then threw his payment on to the sheriff's desk. 'I didn't get Glenn to jail.'

'Escaped?' Roswell said.

'No. Lynched.' Lorimer pointed outside when Roswell only stared at him in horror. 'The body's out at the side. I don't reckon anybody saw me bring it back into town.'

'What happened?'

'I don't know. I did what I told you I'd do and went to Webster's Crossing.' Lorimer rubbed the back of his head and put on a pained expression. 'I was waiting for the train, but the next I knew I was waking up with a sore head and Glenn was swinging from the roof.'

Roswell winced. 'Did you see anyone following you?'

'No. I reckon it was more likely someone was waiting for me.'

Roswell rubbed his jaw as he pondered this point and then frowned.

'That suggests someone heard about the route you'd take.'

'I didn't talk to anyone about my mission.'

Roswell glanced aside, suggesting he had spoken to someone. With it looking as if he might get to leave the law office without being accused of being involved in the incident, Lorimer backed away for a pace.

Roswell joined him in moving on to the door, but when they were outside he turned to Lorimer.

'Don't leave town until I've finished my investigation,' he declared.

Roswell then walked to the side of the law office. Lorimer figured that the less time he spent with Roswell the better, as every time they talked he risked incriminating himself, so he headed to Ewing's saloon.

As he walked to the bar Wheeler looked at him with a surprised expression before scowling, the reason becoming clear when he joined him.

'I've just heard the rumour you took Glenn to jail,' he said. 'I'd never have expected you to do that.'

'I needed the money,' Lorimer said. He glanced around and confirmed that nobody was close enough to hear them talking. 'Don't tell anyone until the word spreads, but he never got there. He got lynched.'

A smile spread across Wheeler's face and he punched the air with glee before he took Lorimer's point that he shouldn't attract attention by making his delight too obvious.

'Who did it?'

'I don't know. I got jumped at Webster's Crossing.'

Wheeler winked. 'I'll believe you, but the more important matter is whether Sheriff Roswell believes you.'

'He's thinking about it. Either way, I didn't get paid.'

'Don't worry about that. After what you did – or I guess after what you failed to do – you get a free room here for as long as you want it and you won't have to pay for another drink.'

'In that case, I'll have a whiskey.'

When Wheeler provided a glass of whiskey, Lorimer turned around and leaned back against the bar to again avoid being drawn into a conversation where he might accidently reveal his guilt. He raised the glass to his lips, but then lowered it without taking a sip and turned back to Wheeler.

'You look troubled,' Wheeler said. 'Don't be. Glenn's not worth it.'

'So he was guilty, then?'

Wheeler slapped a hand to the bar with an emphatic gesture.

'He sure was.'

'Glenn claimed otherwise.' Lorimer raised a hand when Wheeler started to pour scorn on his comment. 'I know I can't trust anything he said, but I wasn't here when it happened, so what was his defence?'

Wheeler sneered. 'It wasn't worth making. The shooting happened outside the forge at Harlow's Bend. He claimed he heard gunfire and saw two men riding away beside the creek. He said he couldn't

51

provide a description as they were too far away, and when other people scouted around they didn't see them.'

Wheeler looked at Lorimer until he nodded and then moved away to deal with a customer. Lorimer swirled his whiskey, but he still didn't take a drink as Wheeler's explanation had set off an alarming train of thought.

Two men had ambushed Manford Wigfall, shot him up and then ridden away. These men had been careful and nobody else had seen them.

This was broadly the same sequence of events that Glenn had described in his defence. Worse, Manford had something in common with Budd.

Ten years ago they had both been involved in the raid on the poker game, albeit with different roles, and they had both testified at the Devlin brothers' trial leading to them getting jailed for nine years.

As this connection felt compelling, Lorimer's hand shook with an involuntary tremor spilling whiskey over the bar. He put down the glass and gulped.

'The Devlin brothers are back,' he said to himself.

CHAPTER 6

Benedict Harlow was standing outside his house when Lorimer rode up from the creek towards him.

The previous night Lorimer had seen Sheriff Roswell head this way so he presumed that Benedict had received the bad news about his son. Lorimer reckoned he wouldn't be welcome, but after reaching a troubling conclusion about Budd's death he had to try to get answers from probably the only person who could provide them.

As it turned out Benedict watched him stop and dismount without showing any sign he would send him on his way.

'I heard what happened yesterday and the part you played,' Benedict said when Lorimer stood in front of him.

'I know I'm the last person you want to see, but I had to come,' Lorimer said. 'I want to apologize for my failing. Then you can knock me down or whatever else you want to do.'

'I don't want anything of you, but I applaud your courage in coming here.' Benedict looked across Harlow's Bend towards Lorimer's old home. 'I remember that when you make a mistake you're honest about what you've done, no matter how hard that makes your life.'

Lorimer was pleased Benedict wasn't facing him as he was sure he must look guilty.

'I'm relieved you see it that way, and if you have any questions I'll try to answer them.'

Benedict looked through the window and then beckoned for Lorimer to follow him inside.

'I don't need to know anything more, but Abigail might.'

Abigail was Christina's older sister and Glenn's widow, so he expected the meeting would be awkward. When they joined her at the kitchen table, she was staring out of the window.

Her gaze was set on the other side of Harlow's Bend, although she wouldn't be able to see her sister's house. She ignored them for a while before facing Lorimer.

'No more visitors,' she murmured and turned away.

'This is Lorimer Hall,' Benedict said. 'You probably remember him. He's just returned to town and Sheriff Roswell hired him to take Glenn to jail. He's come to tell us he's sorry he failed to do that.'

She swirled round and stared at Lorimer with her eyes wide and aghast. Lorimer couldn't tell if she was going to burst out crying or slap him, but in the end she just gave a curt nod.

'Thank you for coming,' she said, her voice small. 'I'm sure you did everything you could. The only men at fault are those who did that wicked act.'

'That's mighty reasonable of you,' Lorimer said. 'In your position I don't reckon I'd have been as charitable.'

She gnawed her bottom lip and, with it not looking as if she would say anything more, he backed away, but then she raised a hand.

'You were the last kindly face Glenn would have seen. Did he say anything?'

'He told me he was innocent.'

'He was, even if nobody believes it.' She snuffled, the tears that he'd expected now brimming. 'Go now. I won't get my husband's body to bury for a while, so it's too soon to talk about this.'

When she turned to the window Lorimer headed to the door. Benedict stayed to speak quietly with her and then followed him.

'I wish I could have said something that was more comforting,' Lorimer said when they were outside.

'You might not think it, but you helped,' Benedict said. 'After Budd's death everyone sided with Christina and we've not been popular. You're one of the few supportive people she's seen, and the fact you were Budd's friend makes your attitude even more welcome.'

'Then maybe I should come back later when she's calmer.'

'You could.' Benedict stood in front of him and set his hands on his hips. 'Or you could just tell me why you really came here.'

Lorimer thought quickly now he'd been invited to ask the questions he had wanted to bring up.

'Your son's death troubles me,' he said after a while. 'It's set my mind whirling.'

'I'm not surprised you're troubled, but I am surprised you took on the assignment, bearing in mind Budd was your friend.'

Lorimer had expected this question, so he had prepared a suitable lie and he had no problem meeting Benedict's eye.

'I wanted to question Glenn as I was unsure of his guilt. I didn't get the chance, but I'm now even more convinced he was innocent.'

Benedict furrowed his brow. 'You weren't in town when Budd died, so what made you think that?'

'I wasn't here two months ago, but I did arrive at the same time as Manford Wigfall was attacked.'

'I heard about that incident and that you tried to help him, but it had nothing to do with Budd's death.'

Lorimer raised a finger. 'Except I reckon it has. They're connected by the incident that made Glenn and Budd feud and made me leave town and made—'

'You're talking about the Devlins' raid?' Benedict snapped, his voice rising with a strong emotion, perhaps shock.

'I sure am.'

Benedict tipped back his hat as he thought this through and then blew out his cheeks in a show of his scepticism.

'So you reckon Reinhold and Griffin Devlin have returned to get revenge on the people who gave evidence at their trial?'

Lorimer nodded, now pleased he'd come here, as he'd hoped Benedict would pour cold water on his theory and help to alleviate his guilt.

'I do. Four men were playing poker in my pa's forge when the Devlins arrived. I was keeping lookout and Budd was holding their horses for their quick escape. Our decision to speak up against them, combined with my father, you and Manford identifying them made the case clear cut.'

'It did, but your tone of voice suggests you regret speaking up.' Benedict frowned when Lorimer didn't reply. 'Then again, you and Budd were treated harshly, bearing in mind you were young and naive.'

Lorimer shook his head, unwilling to accept an excuse for his actions, but he didn't reply immediately as he considered whether he wanted to explain further.

'What still annoys me is that Sheriff O'Toole lied,' he said after a while. 'He said I'd go to prison for ten years, except I wasn't aware that he knew the Devlins had done it and that he wasn't even sure I was involved. If I'd have kept quiet, the brothers would still have gone to jail and me and Budd might not have suffered.'

'You weren't to know that and no matter what the consequences, you did the right thing.'

Lorimer sighed, wondering how he could sum up the last ten years of his life in a few words.

After his part in the raid everyone had treated him as a pariah, his father included. His father had explained that the only thing a man can trust is his own values, and as Lorimer hadn't done that he would have to take his punishment.

The only way he could avoid going bad was to grow up quickly and accept responsibility for his actions. Lorimer reckoned this would be a hard discipline to follow, so he had left home instead.

After that, the effects of his treatment led to him distrusting authority and he got into trouble all on his own. He'd spent time in jail twice for robbery and he'd been involved in several criminal misadventures he'd been lucky to survive.

As he figured that Benedict wouldn't welcome hearing him try to lay the blame for his failings on Sheriff O'Toole, he shrugged.

'Maybe I did, but the question is whether doing the right thing led to Budd being killed.'

Benedict rocked his head from side to side and then nodded.

'It's possible and either way it makes more sense than any other explanation I've considered.'

Benedict moved away and leaned back against the wall as he thought through the implications. Lorimer stood beside him while trying not to let his disappointment show now that Benedict was willing to accept his theory.

'Not that I have any proof,' Lorimer said. 'All I have is that I heard that your son claimed he saw two men riding away from Budd's body, and I saw two men attack Manford and then flee.'

'I know it's only a theory, but if you're right then the other two people who spoke up as witnesses could be their next targets.'

Benedict emphasized his point by pointing at Lorimer and then tapping his own chest. When Lorimer nodded, Benedict turned towards the town as if he was already looking out for signs of trouble.

'So the waiting game begins.'

Benedict nodded. 'It does, so I reckon we should make it easy for them. You'll stay with us.'

Lorimer gulped, not reckoning he could cope with spending time with people he'd deceived about his actions and intentions, but Benedict looked at him earnestly, so he accepted the offer.

'I'll go back to town and collect my belongings. I'll return by sundown. Be careful until then.'

When Benedict went inside to collect a gun, Lorimer headed to his horse and mounted up. Abigail was looking out the window at him and as she appeared calmer, presumably because Benedict had explained what was happening, he rode away with his head bowed.

He dallied in town to ensure he didn't have to return until sundown. He didn't tell Wheeler where he would be staying and the bartender didn't object to his leaving, although as the news of Glenn's demise had now spread he was too busy chatting about the matter with his customers to pay him much attention.

When Lorimer returned to Benedict's house he refused Abigail's offer to eat with them, claiming he wanted to scout around before it got dark so he could get to know the lie of the land. This was a weak excuse as he had grown up on Harlow's Bend, but she didn't object, so he walked down to the creek.

He found a spot by the water where he could keep watch while thinking about a problem that didn't have a solution.

If Reinhold and Griffin Devlin came for him it would go a long way towards proving he had failed Glenn, an innocent man. If they didn't come he would never know for sure whether he had failed an innocent man or a guilty man.

His dwelling on the matter of whether the brothers had returned to Clear Creek turned his thoughts to the other brothers who he did know had caused trouble recently.

For Moody and Vester to have lynched their cousin's husband they must have been sure of his guilt. He doubted they would explain their reasoning, but he still set off towards the other side of Harlow's Bend.

He was some distance from the place when he lost the chance to get an explanation that night; the White brothers and Christina came outside and mounted horses.

They rode off towards town without looking his way. He stopped to consider his next action and then, on a whim, resumed walking.

He moved on to the line of trees that sheltered the graves, by which time the three riders were no longer visible in the deepening gloom. There were four graves, which was two more than he'd expected, although an inscription showed that one of them was Budd's.

He stood in front of Budd's mound, but found that he couldn't stay there, so he walked in front of the other graves. His parents' final resting places were next to each other, and he didn't know who was in the last grave in the line as there was no legend.

He stood beside his father's grave, but as with Budd's grave he couldn't look at it, so he faced the creek.

'It's probably good that you didn't live to see what's happening now,' he said.

He sighed, finding that speaking aloud didn't feel as unnatural as it had done when he'd talked to Glenn's body in the station house.

'You always said that the only thing a man can rely on is his values, but that's turned out to be wrong. The Devlins didn't care about such things back then and they don't care about them now.'

Lorimer lowered his head, wondering if he should speak of the matter that troubled him the most and which he'd never told his father, as he wouldn't have accepted his excuse. Then, figuring he'd never speak of it if he didn't do so now, he cleared his throat and sat down, although he still faced the water.

'I didn't help the Devlins because I was rebelling against the values you tried to instil in me. I followed them. They said that if I didn't help them they'd kill the people closest to me. That was you and Budd. So I got involved and everything went wrong, and it was because I cared too much.'

With that said, he didn't feel any better about having come here to speak his mind. So he stood up and turned upriver as he aimed to go back to Benedict's house before it became fully dark, but for some reason he couldn't take the first step.

'I'm in big trouble, Pa,' he said. 'What you said would happen to me turned out to be right. I got an innocent man killed. If he'd have been guilty, maybe I could have lived with that, but I don't reckon he was and I've got no idea what to do now.'

Lorimer sighed, feeling strangely relieved to have admitted this out loud.

'Be true in everything you do and, no matter what the problem is, it'll work out fine in the end.'

Lorimer flinched. He had spoken aloud, but he had also imagined hearing his father say the words, and that made him so uncomfortable he shivered.

He decided he'd spent enough time indulging in self-pity, but he had to admit he had got an answer. Trying to prove that the Devlins hadn't killed Budd to assuage his guilt might never work, but doing the right thing for his friend by finding out who did kill him, whoever that might be, would give him the certainty he needed.

He moved on to Budd's grave and this time he was able to stand in front of it.

'Goodbye, old friend,' he said.

'I don't reckon he heard you,' a voice said behind him.

The reply was so unexpected that Lorimer gasped and stood rigidly as he wondered if his mind had played another trick on him. He shook off his spooked feeling and turned around, but he walked into a swinging punch to the jaw that sent him reeling backwards until he fell over.

He lay on his back looking up at the dim early evening stars until a man loomed up over him. In the poor light at first he didn't recognize his assailant, and when he placed him he couldn't help but laugh.

'Howdy, Lorimer,' Griffin Devlin said. 'It's been a while.'

CHAPTER 7

Lorimer snaked backwards across the ground as he tried to move away from Griffin, but the man followed him.

Then Griffin's brother, Reinhold, stepped into his line of sight. Reinhold stood on the other side of him with a hand resting on his holster.

'Do you often talk to yourself?' he asked.

'I get better conversation that way,' Lorimer said and laughed again.

'What in tarnation are you finding funny?'

'I stopped caring about proving you'd not returned to Clear Creek. Then you turned up. It almost makes me believe in miracles.'

Reinhold shook his head. Then he reached down, slapped his hands on Lorimer's shoulders and lifted him up from the ground.

'You're not making no sense. I hope that'll change.'

Reinhold rolled his shoulders and bunched a fist, so Lorimer tried to push him away, but that made Griffin hurry forward. Griffin stood behind him and removed Lorimer's gun, but as he threw the weapon aside Lorimer jerked his elbow back into his opponent's stomach.

Griffin groaned and stepped to the side while doubling over. Fortunately for Lorimer he bumped into Reinhold, so Lorimer took advantage and while Reinhold was off-balance he hammered a lowered shoulder into his chest.

The blow knocked Reinhold back for a pace after which Lorimer kept moving. Reinhold and Griffin made to grab him and Reinhold caught a fleeting hold of his arm, but he shook off the hand and broke into a run.

He went pounding down towards the creek. A few moments later his opponents muttered to each other and gave chase.

Several boulders were by the water's edge, and with the moon being behind a band of low cloud Lorimer reckoned he might find a pool of darkness there in which to hide. He ran on, leaping over small rocks and weaving around bushes.

He didn't look back to see how close his pursuers were, but their harsh breathing was so loud they were probably only a few feet behind him. He was twenty paces from the water's edge and even closer to a boulder when a grunt sounded a moment before Griffin slammed into his side, making him stumble.

Unable to control himself, Lorimer tipped over and crashed down on the sloping ground on his front. Then he went sliding along until he clattered into the boulder.

Griffin fetched up beside him, but he had less luck than Lorimer had and banged his head against the rock. With Griffin rubbing his brow and Reinhold still hurrying down the slope, Lorimer scrambled to his feet and rounded the boulder.

Ahead was the creek. The water's edge to the right was open for some distance while three large rocks blocked the route to the left.

He could probably find somewhere to go to ground amongst the rocks, so he went in the other direction, figuring his unexpected action might confuse his pursuers.

He scurried along with his head down to keep out of the brothers' sight and then threw himself to the ground at the side of the boulder. Reinhold then came around the boulder and murmured in irritation as he skidded to a halt.

He called to Griffin who took a few moments to join him. Then all was silent.

As Lorimer couldn't see the men he hoped they were trying to work out where he had hidden himself near the water's edge.

Increasing the possibility that he had, in fact,

confounded them, receding footfalls sounded.

'He can't have gone far,' Griffin said. 'I'll keep watch and you take them one at a time.'

Lorimer assumed Reinhold would explore behind each large rock and in the gloom he would probably take some time. When he failed to find him it was likely they'd then discover his hiding place, so Lorimer got up on to his haunches and faced the route up the slope towards the graves.

He would have to move over open ground, but even in the short time since Reinhold and Griffin had jumped him the darkness had grown deeper.

With his body doubled over he shuffled towards the graves. He kept one eye on the scene at the water's edge, but he couldn't see the men.

With every step his hopes grew that he might get away, or at least put some distance between him and the men before he was seen. By the time he reached the mounds he felt confident he had escaped unseen.

He looked for his gun that had been taken earlier, but he failed to find it and, with the urgent need to move on, he abandoned the search and stood on the other side of the trees. He considered whether to head to Benedict's house or seek refuge beside the nearer house.

The forge door was open and as this would provide the closest decent cover, he hurried there. He reached his destination without mishap and slipped in through the door to stand in the darkness where he looked around choosing his next place to head for.

He had yet to decide which direction to go when something scraped across the floor behind him. Before he could react, a chain swung down past his face and clattered on to his chest.

The chain was drawn up tight to his throat and he was yanked backwards.

'The darkness hid you, but that works both ways,' Griffin muttered in his ear.

Griffin then swung him round to face the dark interior of the forge. Lorimer discerned Reinhold, presumably, moving around in the gloom.

A creaking noise sounded and light flared, illuminating Reinhold's face. Reinhold was peering into a long, open-topped firebox as he raked through the embers of the fire that would have been used earlier in the day.

When he'd encouraged flames to rise up he warmed his hands and then turned to Lorimer.

'Bring him over here,' he said. 'I'll do the questioning.'

Griffin shoved Lorimer forward. Lorimer stood his ground, but when Griffin gave the chain around his neck a warning tug he moved on.

'What do you two want to know?' Lorimer said when he had been positioned in front of Reinhold.

'That's the first sensible thing you've said. I hope

that continues. You were with Manford so you made it impossible for us to get answers out of him, but that's not a problem as I reckon you know what we want.'

Lorimer shrugged. 'I reckon you want to talk about what happened in here ten years ago.'

Reinhold smiled and then looked around the forge. His gaze took in the far corner where the poker game had taken place before he faced a line of ironwork that had been propped up against a wall.

He moved away and walked along, examining each length of metal until he selected a branding iron with a grunt of satisfaction, his action making Lorimer tense up. Griffin noticed his concern and laughed.

'Don't worry,' he muttered in Lorimer's ear. 'If you're co-operative, this won't hurt.'

Reinhold walked back to the firebox and thrust the end of the iron into the glowing embers.

'If you're not, it sure will,' he said with a smirk.

Reinhold set about stoking the fire, and although Lorimer tried not to pay attention to his activities, he couldn't help but watch the flames grow stronger.

'Ask your questions now,' he said with a gulp.

Reinhold ignored him as he concentrated on the iron and when he deemed that it was hot enough, he raised it up. The brand was a capital T and the letter glowed red in the gloom within the darkened forge.

'So what could the T stand for?' Reinhold turned to Lorimer and passed the brand from hand to hand. 'Could it be traitor, or turncoat, or maybe Templeman?'

Lorimer had been shaking his head, but the final option made him frown.

'Who's Templeman?'

'And there's the question we're here to answer.'

'Then I can't answer it as I've got no idea who this person is.'

Even as he uttered his denial he recalled hearing the name before, although he couldn't remember when. With Reinhold standing before him holding a glowing brand, he struggled to make himself think of anything other than what might happen next.

Reinhold appeared to pick up on his thoughts as he swung the brand away and thrust it back into the fire. Then he came back and spread Lorimer's jacket before raising his vest to expose his belly.

'You have one minute to remember. Then you'll get a permanent reminder.'

Bearing Manford's fate in mind, Lorimer doubted that an answer would lead to him being freed, but he tried to concentrate on recalling when he'd heard the name before. For these men to be asking about it and for him to recognize it, it had to have been when he'd last been here, and that conclusion led him to the answer.

He sighed with relief. 'Carl Templeman. . . . you're talking about Carl Templeman?'

'I sure am. Tell me about him.'

Lorimer shrugged. 'It was just a name I once heard. He played poker here with Manford Wigfall, Benedict Harlow and my father.'

'That's a good start.' Reinhold raked the brand through the embers for emphasis. 'Tell me more.'

'There is no more. I never met him and he didn't come forward at your trial, so I assume he left town.'

Reinhold brought the brand out of the firebox using a slow movement that fixed Lorimer's attention on the glowing end. Then, with the brand thrust out, he moved towards Lorimer, who cringed back against his captor, but Reinhold stopped with the end still a foot away from his flesh.

'Keep assuming.'

'I'd never heard of him before the game so I assume he didn't come from Clear Creek, and I guess what you did scared him so he stayed out of your way.'

Reinhold raised an eyebrow, requesting more, but no matter how hard he thought about it he couldn't recall anything else about a man who had just been a name mentioned in passing ten years earlier. He shook his head, making Reinhold frown.

'Scream as loud as you like,' he said. 'Then we'll

start at the beginning again.'

Reinhold winked and then inched the brand towards him.

CHAPTER 8

'You have to believe me,' Lorimer said, speaking quickly. 'There's nothing more, but tell me why you're interested in Carl Templeman and maybe that'll help me to remember something.'

Reinhold stopped moving the brand, leaving it only inches from Lorimer's skin. It was so close the heat radiating from its fiery end made him draw in his stomach while an acrid smell invaded his nostrils that he feared was body hair fizzling away.

Reinhold then looked at Griffin, presumably as he asked silently whether he should respond. Griffin moved slightly and his reaction made Reinhold look at the door.

A few moments later a noise could be heard outside, and although Lorimer couldn't work out what it was, Reinhold withdrew the brand and headed to the door.

Lorimer figured that this distraction would give him his best chance of breaking free, so when

Reinhold peered outside he turned his head. He watched Reinhold, making it appear that he was as interested in what was happening outside as the brothers were.

When Griffin shifted position so he could keep an eye on the situation, too, Lorimer stepped back and barged into his captor. The tight chain around his neck loosened, so he thrust up an arm and grabbed a handful of links.

Lorimer braced himself and then jerked forward while bending over double. Griffin went sprawling on to his back and released the chain, so Lorimer twisted to the side while pushing up.

The weight buckled his knees before his captor went crashing down on his side and rolled away from him.

Lorimer stumbled and went to his knees while from the corner of his eye he saw Reinhold rushing towards him. In desperation he yanked the chain from around his neck and turned to him.

As Reinhold advanced, Lorimer rose up and swung the chain from side to side as he prepared to swipe whichever one of his opponents came closest. Reinhold glanced at Griffin, who was showing no sign of making a move on him, and then with a snarl of irritation he hurled the brand at Lorimer.

The glowing end hurtled through the air towards his chest, and with only a moment to react, Lorimer raised the coiled loops of chain while turning and backing away. A clang sounded as the brand scraped across the chain and Lorimer felt a sharp pain in his ribs.

He continued to move away and squirmed. When the pain didn't worsen he looked down and to his relief the brand was lying smouldering on the floor. Then he looked up and it was to find that Griffin and Reinhold were beating a hasty retreat.

They were hurrying towards the far corner of the forge. In anger at his treatment Lorimer set off after them, but when they ran through the back door and into the darkness beyond he slowed to a halt.

He threw the chain to the floor and felt his chest. He located a sore spot, but the burn was small and, figuring he'd got out of a tricky situation in better condition than he'd feared, he walked to the main door.

When he looked out he saw the reason for the noise that had worried his captors. The White brothers had returned.

They were striding towards the forge while Christina and Sheriff Roswell were a hundred yards away and riding towards the house.

'You waited until we left home so you could snoop around,' Moody said with a raised voice.

'Quit shouting at me,' Lorimer said, gesturing into the forge. 'Two men accosted me and they're getting away.'

His plea didn't slow down either man and they

advanced on him with menace. They were five paces away when Lorimer accepted they wouldn't listen to reason and hurried back into the forge.

He scurried to the chain and picked it up. When he turned around both men were almost upon him, so he swung the chain at the nearest man, Moody, who stopped and flinched away, his quick action letting him avoid it.

Vester was more circumspect. He watched the moving chain and when it clattered against the firebox he stepped in.

Lorimer swung the chain backhanded towards his opponent, but he was too slow and Vester reached him before he could be hit. Then, with a raised forearm, Vester bundled him away, making him crash into the firebox.

Lorimer dropped the chain, and before he could reclaim it Vester grabbed his shoulders, doubled him over, and thrust his face down towards the burning embers.

'What are you doing here?' Vester demanded.

'I told you what. . . .' Lorimer trailed off when the hot air made him cough and the pungent smoke made his eyes water.

'We saw the smoke even in the dark. We know you've been up to no good, so tell me what you were doing and you won't be eating fire.'

Lorimer tried to speak, but another bout of coughing made that impossible. Then thankfully

Sheriff Roswell spoke up from the doorway.

'Let him go,' he said. 'I don't reckon he had enough time to do any damage.'

Vester held on to Lorimer for several more moments. Then with a grunt of irritation he raised his head and threw him aside.

Lorimer went down on his hands and knees where he stared at the floor with his vision blurred while he fought to stop coughing. When he could breathe normally again he straightened up.

Vester and Moody had gone outside while Roswell was standing over him with his arms folded. He had a thunderous expression, just like everyone else who had confronted him this evening.

'I'm obliged you helped me,' Lorimer said as he stood up. 'Two men attacked me and dragged me in here. I reckon they're the men who killed Manford Wigfall. They can't have gone far.'

Lorimer pointed at the back door, but Roswell continued to glare at him.

'I can't see no reason to trust the word of a liar,' he said.

'What do you mean?'

Roswell advanced a short pace on him.

'I've been asking around about you. You said you were only a relative of Jeremiah Hall, but you're his son!'

Lorimer shrugged. 'I didn't think it was important and I assumed you must have checked up on me before giving me the assignment.'

'My only mistake was trusting you were a decent man, but you knew Glenn Harlow. I was especially interested to hear about the incident that forced you to leave town, along with your friendship with Budd Ewing, a man whose killer is now dead because you failed to carry out your duty.'

Lorimer spread his hands and tried to placate Roswell with a smile.

'I know that looks suspicious, but I didn't kill Glenn. Heck, I'm staying with Benedict and Abigail Harlow.'

Roswell shook his head. 'Then what I heard about you is right. You're a twisted man who's not to be trusted.'

'I have no plans, twisted or otherwise. I returned to Clear Creek because I'd heard my father had died, and while I was here I found out my old friend was dead. If you hadn't have asked me to take Glenn to jail I'd have left town and you'd never have seen me again.'

'Except I did ask, and right now things are looking bad for you. You're the only witness to what happened to Manford and nobody else has seen the men you claimed killed him.'

Lorimer opened his mouth to continue claiming his innocence, but then decided not to waste his breath, as the sheriff clearly wouldn't believe anything he said.

'You may not trust me, but don't dismiss what I reckon is happening. The men who attacked me are the Devlin brothers.'

'They were your partners in crime that you turned against!' Roswell tipped back his hat while directing an exasperated glare at him. 'I guess I can't blame them for wanting to harm you.'

Lorimer ignored Roswell's scornful attitude and looked him in the eye.

'If you accept that, accept that they would also want to harm Manford, and maybe even Budd Ewing before that.'

Roswell muttered something under his breath and, confirming his patience had worn out, he grabbed Lorimer's arm and escorted him out of the forge. Outside, the White brothers were standing at the door to the house, and when Roswell paused to gesture to them they acknowledged him with nods and went inside.

Roswell held on to Lorimer for another minute while they walked away. Then he threw him forward.

'Go back to Benedict, but don't harm him or his family and don't get too comfortable, as when I've learnt everything I can about you, I reckon I'll be coming for you.'

Lorimer didn't retort and Roswell's threat made him trudge back towards Benedict's house. His route took him past the trees and when he reached them he looked over his shoulder.

Roswell was heading to his horse and he didn't appear to be watching him leave, so Lorimer slipped through the trees to the mounds.

This time he was lucky as the moon emerged from behind a cloud and a gleam of light on the ground let him locate his gun. He then stood for a while on the spot where he'd gathered a sense of purpose before the Devlins had attacked him.

In a thoughtful frame of mind, he walked down to the water's edge where he withdrew the money the White brothers had given him at Webster's Crossing and hurled it into the water.

Then he took hold of the stolen watch and moved to send it after the money, but the sheen on the metal made him stay his hand as he recalled another occasion when he might have come across Templeman's name. He peered at the back of the watch, but he couldn't read the inscription that he'd only glanced at before.

He turned the watch in several directions until he found an angle that made the lettering stand out. The sight confirmed his suspicion and made him gasp.

The dedication claimed that the watch had been a gift from Jessica Templeman.

CHAPTER 9

When Lorimer returned to Benedict's house, Benedict came out and met him at the door.

'I thought I heard some trouble on the other side of the bend,' Benedict said.

'There was and I was involved,' Lorimer said. 'The Devlin brothers jumped me. I didn't get a chance to question them about Budd and things were looking bad, but then Sheriff Roswell arrived and they ran.'

Benedict peered past him as if he might still catch sight of the Devlins.

'Then I'm sorry I wasn't there to help, but at least we know for sure they're back. Even better, the sheriff knows about it.'

Lorimer didn't reply until he'd headed inside and joined Abigail, who was sitting at the table near the window. She must have heard the conversation as she looked at him with a hopeful expression, making Lorimer take a deep breath before he dashed her hopes.

'I'm sorry, but what just happened isn't good news. Sheriff Roswell now knows I was Budd's friend and he no longer trusts me. So he didn't believe my theory that the Devlins killed Budd, or even that they're back.'

Abigail slapped the table in frustration while Benedict dragged out a chair from under the table so quickly the wood creaked and then threw himself down on to it.

'So nobody wants to believe in my son's innocence,' Benedict said. 'And the Devlins are still looking for revenge.'

'That sums it up, and there's a new mystery. The Devlins are looking for Carl Templeman.'

Benedict firmed his jaw and Abigail exhaled sharply. They turned to each other and their eyes met before Benedict got up and went to the window and Abigail lowered her head.

Lorimer waited for an explanation for their reactions, but when Benedict turned away from the window he pointed to the door.

'I'll keep watch outside for a while in case they come,' he said. 'Abigail set your dinner aside, so eat that. Then tonight we'll all listen out for trouble.'

Lorimer nodded, but he didn't reply until Benedict reached the door.

'Why do you reckon they're interested in Carl?'

he asked.

Benedict stopped in the doorway and shrugged.

'I don't know,' he said and then went outside.

Lorimer turned to Abigail, but she got up and busied herself with warming up tonight's meal for him. With a sigh he accepted they didn't want to talk about this subject, and he got further proof when she handed him a plate and then left him alone.

He ate while thinking through the events of the day and his thoughts soon turned to wondering why the watch he'd taken from Manford was a gift from Jessica Templeman, who was presumably a close relative of Carl's. He couldn't come up with a theory, so he tried to recall the little he'd heard about this man, hoping that now he was no longer facing a fraught situation he might drag up more details.

He couldn't remember anything else, although he recalled that Sheriff O'Toole had told him the little he did know when he'd questioned him in the law office.

An hour later, when Benedict returned, he was still sitting at the table.

'What happened to Sheriff O'Toole?' he asked.

He looked at Benedict with a blank expression in the hope that he wouldn't work out he was asking because of his connection to a man he didn't want to talk about.

'Finlay retired with distinction and we all wished

him well,' Benedict said. 'He lives a couple of hours upriver now.'

'In that case, can you keep watch here tomorrow while I go to see him?'

'I can,' Benedict said cautiously.

Lorimer spread his hands. 'Sheriff Roswell won't be pleased I've left town, even for a short while, so make an excuse if he comes here.'

Benedict moved closer to him. 'I'll do that, but what's so important that you have to see Finlay?'

'He knows the Devlins better than anyone. Maybe he can work out what they'll do next, or at the least he might talk to Roswell and convince him to take the threat seriously.'

Benedict jutted his jaw as he thought this through and then gave a curt nod, his slow response suggesting he was still wary of Lorimer's motivation in seeking out the former lawman. Then they settled down for the night.

Lorimer refused the offer to take a room at the back of the house. Instead he sat in a chair near to the door where he could respond quickly if anything happened overnight.

As it turned out, the night passed peacefully. In the morning he got ready to leave without delay, figuring he should see Finlay and then return quickly to both help Benedict keep guard and to reduce the likelihood of Roswell finding out he'd gone.

To his surprise, before he'd mounted up, Abigail

came out to join him and she was dressed to travel.

'I'm coming with you,' she said.

'Why?' Lorimer said with an exasperated shake of the head.

'While I wait to bury my husband I can't spend every waking hour hoping my sister will come walking across the bend to see me, and I'll be safer with you than with my father-in-law as when I'm travelling I'm less likely to meet the Devlins.'

'That's by no means certain.' Lorimer waved his arms as he tried to think of a better reason to dissuade her. 'I'm sure Benedict would agree.'

He looked at the house in the hope of attracting Benedict's attention, but she shook her head.

'He agreed with me that I need to hear whatever Finlay has to say about the Devlins.'

'And about anything else he says?' Lorimer said as he now got a clue about why she wanted to join him.

'Of course. Now, are we leaving or are we going to waste the day talking?'

Lorimer sighed. 'I guess we're leaving.'

With that he turned away and mounted up. He didn't wait for her and rode off towards the creek.

He hoped that she'd misrepresented the situation and that once Benedict spotted what she was doing he'd call her back, but before he reached the water she came trotting after him. Then they rode together beside the water heading upriver.

'I guess you've already figured out that Carl Templeman interests me,' she said after a few miles. 'But I'm not keeping anything from you as I don't know why he's important.'

'I believe you, but what interests you enough to make this journey?'

Abigail rocked her head from side to side as she appeared to choose her words carefully.

'I overheard Budd and Glenn arguing about this man. I didn't hear enough to work out what the problem was, but it might explain why Budd was killed.'

'What was said about him at the trial?'

'His name never came up. The trial concentrated on the reason for the killing, both the known facts and the scurrilous rumours.'

Abigail glared at him, her stern gaze warning him that she didn't want to discuss the matter further. In deference to her silent plea he didn't respond for several minutes and then he used a low voice.

'I'm sorry, but I need to know what was said.'

Abigail sighed and she rode on for a while before replying.

'It's well known that Benedict and your father argued, as did Budd and Glenn. Nobody knew which feud came first, but they both revolved around Budd's involvement in the raid on the forge and Benedict getting shot.'

'I've heard about some of that. My father was a

placid man, but stern. I can see him bearing a grudge, especially after I left and he started drinking.'

He smiled, hoping she might offer an alternative explanation for his behavior that didn't lay the blame on his leaving, but she only nodded.

'Many people reckoned there was more to it than that. They said the arguments between the two men were over me and Christina. People said both men reckoned they'd picked the wrong sister.'

'It's none of my business, but I assume the rumours were just gossip?'

'You're right. It's none of your business.' She looked at the creek, but then glanced at him. 'Me and Budd rarely spoke even before things turned bad and we had no interest in each other.'

Lorimer noted she had denied only half of the rumour, but as her last comment had been spoken with a raised voice he didn't question whether the other half was valid.

'That's a lot of different versions of events, but if it helps, Glenn told me the bad blood was because he was angry that his father got shot and he blamed Budd.'

'It does help,' she said and then looked at him with an eager expression as she clearly hoped to hear more about his time with her husband.

Lorimer winced. Since he'd decided to get to the truth he had kept his guilty feelings at bay, but now his guts rumbled so he edged his horse on ahead of her to curtail their conversation.

She speeded up to keep abreast of him and as they rode in silence she looked thoughtful, suggesting she had noticed his rebuff. That didn't stop him dwelling on the fact that his mission to see Finlay might turn out to be another step towards proving he had ruined her life.

For the next two hours they spoke only when she pointed out landmarks that marked their progress. She had just reported that they were a half-hour away from their destination when Lorimer noticed a bigger problem.

They were being followed.

CHAPTER 10

Lorimer avoided looking over his shoulder and used the changes in direction when they skirted around the side of the winding creek to look back in a natural manner.

They had only one follower, an observation that made him relax as he reckoned the Devlins wouldn't have split up. With it being more likely that the follower was Sheriff Roswell, a man he didn't welcome meeting, he relayed his concern to Abigail and that they should speed up, but she only furrowed her brow.

'That's nothing to worry about,' she said. 'Plenty of people come this way.'

He sighed, accepting his dark mood had stopped him from considering that being followed could be an innocent happenstance. He tried to foster a calmer mood by slowing down and over the next few miles the rider gained on them.

Abigail's reports on their progress suggested they would soon see Finlay's house, thereby arriving at their destination before the rider reached them, but then hoofbeats pounded behind him. Lorimer looked back and confirmed the follower had broken into a gallop.

He turned to Abigail, but she was staring ahead while sporting a shocked expression. When he saw the reason he joined her in being concerned.

A second rider was heading towards them and this man was clearly Griffin Devlin. Lorimer glanced back and in the last few moments the other rider had come close enough to let him see it was Reinhold.

'Head to the water's edge,' he called to Abigail.

'We'll get trapped there,' she said, shaking her head. 'We should make a run for Finlay's house.'

She gestured ahead and, figuring she knew the area better than he did, he beckoned for her to pick a route. She speeded up to a fast trot and rode towards Griffin, a move that at first looked foolhardy, but when Lorimer hurried his horse on and drew alongside her he saw that she was aiming to reach a long, narrow mound before Griffin did.

Sure enough, as she approached the end of the mound she swung away from the creek and pounded along, taking a route inland that kept the mound to their left and even higher ground to their right. A hundred yards on Lorimer checked on their pursuers and found that Reinhold was approaching the end of the mound, but he was slowing down, presumably to wait for Griffin.

Cheered by this observation Lorimer rode on, and when he next checked on the situation behind them Reinhold had stopped. He whooped with delight, making Abigail glance back and join him in looking pleased, but then Lorimer had an alarming thought.

When the brothers had attacked Manford Wigfall they'd surprised him by coming from an unexpected direction. He glanced around and figured the higher ground inland would be hard to climb, so if Griffin had doubled back with the intention of riding around the mound in the opposite direction, he and Reinhold would trap them.

'Head to the creek,' he called to Abigail. Then, not giving her time to consider his order, he drew his horse to a halt and turned to the mound.

As he picked a route up the slope, she stopped and gestured at him, but then with a sudden movement she rode towards him. The reason became clear when he saw that Reinhold was now riding towards them, possibly confirming their plan.

Lorimer tracked to either side as he gained height with Abigail slipping in behind him. When they approached the summit of the mound, Reinhold was also working his way upwards and he was gesturing, presumably to Griffin, who was out of

Lorimer's line of sight.

They rode over the summit until the creek became visible. Abigail looked upriver and then pointed at a distant green patch.

'That's where Finlay lives,' she said.

'It's some distance away, but if we're lucky we can reach it,' he said.

He pointed, indicating a route down the creekside of the mound that looked gentle enough to traverse at speed. She didn't object so they headed along the summit for a short distance and then moved to lower ground.

The rounded summit now hid Reinhold and he hadn't seen Griffin for some time, so Lorimer's hopes grew that they could evade them for long enough to complete the dash to Finlay's house. Abigail took a different path down and she reached level ground before he did.

Lorimer waved her on and she galloped off, getting a lead of a hundred yards before he could give chase. As he speeded to a gallop he glanced around, again failing to see their pursuers.

The route ahead took them between the creek and the mound, and the end of the mound was a quarter-mile ahead. He figured it would be a dangerous moment when she passed this point as Griffin had probably gone there when he had tried to cut them off, but then, belying his theory, Griffin rode out from a recess in the mound.

He emerged only ten yards ahead of Abigail and his appearance was so sudden it made Abigail's mount rear up. Abigail screeched as with a flailing of her arms she struggled to keep her balance, but then her horse skittered off to the side and that made her tip over and crash to the ground.

Griffin was also struggling to control his mount as it tried to avoid Abigail and her spooked horse, so Lorimer slowed down and then leapt to the ground. He hurried on to Abigail and, as he reached her, she sat up.

'I'm fine,' she said, waving him away. 'Get my horse and we—'

A gunshot rattled. Lorimer looked up, expecting that Griffin had fired, but he had his back to them as he calmed his horse. So he turned to the mound where Reinhold was in a commanding position, sitting astride his horse and aiming his gun down at them.

'No time for that,' Lorimer said and then drew his gun.

He blasted a quick shot that only hit dirt, but was close enough to Reinhold to make him cringe down and hold his fire. Lorimer holstered his gun and took her arm.

She didn't object as he helped her to her feet. Then, with their heads down, they scurried down the sloping ground that led to the creek.

At first she walked with a hobbling gait, but when

Reinhold fired again, his shots slicing into the ground to either side of them, she moved with more urgency.

They headed towards a line of low-lying rocks that protruded from the shallows, this being the only available cover. On the run they waded into the water until they were thigh-deep and then ducked down without Reinhold firing at them again.

Lorimer risked looking up and found that Reinhold was riding down the mound while Griffin was watching them from the top of the slope down to the creek.

'Do you reckon Finlay will have heard the gunfire?' Abigail asked.

'I reckon we're too far away,' Lorimer said. 'We need to figure a way out of this by ourselves.'

His previous encounter with these men meant he reckoned their only hope was to shoot their way out, but he looked at Abigail, giving her a chance to offer an alternative.

'I can't think of one,' she said. 'I've never been in a situation like this before.'

'In that case, keep still and I'll run them off. If I fail, get to your horse and head for Finlay's house while making as much noise as you can.'

He gave an encouraging smile and then put a hand on her shoulder to shift her position and ensure she was below the top of the boulder. His attempt to assure her didn't work as she looked at him with worried eyes, but he still shuffled along behind the boulders to reach the endmost one.

He darted up and glanced around, but he didn't see the brothers and ducked back down. He directed a shrug at Abigail before rising up and snaking his way on to the top of the rock.

While lying on his chest he peered at the nearby terrain seeking out likely places where the gunmen could have gone to ground. The line of rocks in the water was the only obvious cover, but he couldn't see the horses or the recess where Griffin had surprised Abigail, so he figured the men had enough room to lie down beyond the top of the slope.

With this conclusion made he snaked across the rock and lowered himself into the knee-deep water beyond. He picked out a route that would take him to a point ten yards to the side of the last place he'd seen Griffin.

He shuffled along with his head down for around ten yards. Then he stopped to consider the terrain and figured he'd have to climb for another twenty yards before he saw his targets.

A blast of gunfire broke the silence, making Lorimer throw himself on to his front. The shot had been fired from above, but he couldn't tell where it'd been aimed.

Cautiously he raised his head but another shot blasted, making him flinch. This time he saw dirt kick up a few feet ahead of him.

He couldn't see the shooter, so he figured the gunman couldn't see him and he was trying his luck and firing blind. As that policy would probably hit him eventually, Lorimer raised his gun and fired two rapid shots up the slope.

The reports were still echoing when he got up on to his haunches and set off. He holstered his gun in case he needed his hands to scramble up the slope and then pounded along while looking for the first hint of either of the gunmen.

He was ten paces from the top when Reinhold's head and shoulders appeared to his left, and he was aiming his gun at the place where Lorimer had been a few moments earlier. On the run, Lorimer reached for his gun, but he had yet to touch leather when he saw Griffin only a few feet ahead.

The man had been kneeling down in a hollow and his startled expression showed he hadn't heard him approaching. Griffin got over his shock first and he leapt forward, grabbing Lorimer around the shoulders and tipping him over on to his back.

Lorimer slid backwards with Griffin bearing down on him. Lorimer kicked and lashed out, and he managed to jab an elbow into the ground and still his progress.

With his back braced, he hurled Griffin to the side, but his opponent kept hold of him and dragged him on to his side, too. Then both men went tumbling down the slope in a tangle of arms and legs.

After a few rolls the hold each of them had on the other came loose and they separated. Lorimer rolled several more times before he was able to bring himself to a halt.

He lay on his back looking up at the sky that appeared to be still spinning around him. With a shake of the head he tried to control his disorientated feeling and sat up.

He was lying only two yards away from the water's edge. Griffin had rolled further and he was lying on his front in the shallows.

Lorimer scrambled towards him. Griffin saw him coming and pushed himself up on to his knees, but after his tumble Lorimer's gait was uncertain and he stumbled.

As Lorimer pitched forward Griffin rose up to meet him and the two men slammed into each other. Lorimer's momentum forced Griffin to take backwards steps until he reached one of the low-lying rocks.

Lorimer kept pushing forcing Griffin's upper body back over the rock, but his opponent braced himself and then hammered a flailing punch into Lorimer's chest that knocked him to the side. Then Griffin came up behind him and bent him over the rock.

With his feet set wide apart Lorimer strained, stilling his movement before his face reached the rock, and then pushed back until he managed to stand upright. Then the two men tussled.

Using the back of his hand, Griffin slapped Lorimer's cheek and Lorimer retaliated with a swinging uppercut to his opponent's chin before their blows became more frantic and less well-aimed. Their actions slammed them both into the rock and they rolled on to it.

A moment later they tipped over the other side, landing in the water with a splash. Lorimer went under the water and he flailed wildly until he gained his feet, standing up at the same time as Griffin did.

Both men squared off against each other and traded punches. With their clothing drenched and impeding their movements they both landed only weak blows.

Griffin muttered in irritation and pushed Lorimer aside before backing away into deeper water. Lorimer started to follow him, but then saw that Griffin's intention was to give himself room to go for his gun.

On the second attempt Griffin dragged his gun from its holster, but when he raised it, as with the blows they had exchanged, his drenched jacket got in the way. Lorimer threw his hand to his holster and he had more luck, drawing his gun and aiming it at Griffin without being impeded.

With a quick motion he fired, the lead slicing

into Griffin's chest. A pained expression flashed across Griffin's face as he stood up straight, his gun falling from his hand before he toppled over backwards into the water.

He went under, water rising up around him, and when he bobbed back up he was face down. Slowly he drifted away while Lorimer kept his gun trained on him.

He reckoned Griffin was probably dead, but with one problem resolved he accepted with a wince that he still had to deal with the other brother. He turned around and his fears were justified as Reinhold had come down the slope.

Reinhold was now standing on one of the low-lying rocks and he had already aimed his gun at him.

CHAPTER 11

'You shot him!' Reinhold shouted.

'It was self-defence,' Lorimer said.

'We only followed you to get answers, but that doesn't matter none now.'

Reinhold raised his gun to sight Lorimer's head, so in desperation Lorimer gestured at Griffin's body, which was drifting into the middle of the creek.

'You'll never reach him, but I can still save him.'

Lorimer doubted that, but Reinhold glanced at the body and edged forward on to his toes as if he was working out whether he could leap into the water and wade out to his brother before the current took him away. He settled back down and nodded.

'Get him here quickly with no tricks.'

Reinhold thrust his gun arm out as a warning of

what would happen if he took advantage of the reprieve.

'No tricks,' Lorimer said in all honesty, as he had just seen something he hadn't noticed before.

Abigail was no longer hiding in the shallows.

He couldn't see where she was now, but he hoped she had taken heed of his final order and was going back to her horse before embarking on a speedy journey to Finlay's house. He holstered his gun and waded sideways through the water after the body so the current would work with him while he kept one eye on Reinhold.

His hopes were soon dashed. Abigail was behind the rocks and was sneaking up on Reinhold from behind.

He doubted he could stop her from doing something foolish as any signal he might make would attract Reinhold's attention, so he moved slower. He'd taken another three paces and Abigail had reached the boulder on which Reinhold was standing when, with a snarl, Reinhold gestured at him.

'Go faster,' he shouted. 'He's getting further away.'

'It's hard to move through the deeper water,' Lorimer said gesturing with his arms held high to emphasize he was up to his chest in the water.

'Then swim after him.'

Lorimer stayed where he was as Abigail had used the moment of distraction while they'd been talking

to clamber up on to the boulder. She was now standing behind Reinhold clutching a rock.

Reinhold glared at Lorimer, his face reddening
with frustration. Lorimer could see he was unwilling
to shoot him, as he was the only one who could help
his brother, but neither could he let his defiance
continue.

Reinhold appeared to make a decision when he
turned slightly and closed an eye as he sighted
Lorimer, his firm jaw showing he would fire in a
matter of moments. Abigail must have picked up on
his intention as she darted towards him.

At the last moment Reinhold registered the
danger he was in and jerked away from her, but he
was too late. She crunched the rock against his
temple, sending Reinhold crashing down onto the
boulder before toppling off it.

He landed in the shallows on his back and
ploughed through the water for several yards before
he came to a halt. With an uncertain movement he
got back on his feet, stumbled for a few paces into
deeper water before again crashing down on his
back with his arms spread out.

This time he didn't try to gain his feet and he
floated along. The current took him on a path that
was nearer to the side of the creek than Griffin's body
had taken and was around ten yards from Lorimer.

Reinhold looked as if he'd been knocked unconscious, but Lorimer watched him intently. As

Reinhold moved past him, a ripple in the water rocked his body and he tipped over on to his front.

Lorimer glanced at the other body, which was now in the middle of the creek and moving along quickly, so he figured he couldn't have caught up with it even if he'd wanted to. Then he turned to Abigail, who was watching the bodies float away with her mouth open wide in horror.

He waded towards her and she had yet to move when he climbed up on to the boulder and stood beside her. Only then did she cast him a worried glance and drop the rock.

The rock clattered down on to the boulder and skittered along before splashing into the water, both sounds making her flinch as she continued to peer anxiously downwards. He placed a hand on her shoulder and when she edged closer to him he wrapped his arm around her other shoulder.

Abigail gave a wan smile before resting her head against his chest.

'He's dead, isn't he?' she said.

It had been over a minute since Reinhold had rolled over to lie face down in the water, but Lorimer just gripped her shoulder more tightly. He watched the bodies until he could no longer see them amidst the choppy water further down the creek and then turned to her.

'You saved my life,' he said.

'I did, but only by taking another. They could

104

have killed Budd and let Glenn take the blame, but that doesn't make me feel any better.'

'You did what you had to do and I'll never forget that.'

'Neither will I, but for all the wrong reasons.' She gulped and looked him in the eye. 'Before today have you ever had to kill anyone?'

'I haven't,' he said, although his gruff voice made her frown before she returned to watching the water.

They stood for several minutes and long after the possibility had passed that they would see either man again. Then he turned her away from the water and escorted her back up the slope.

When they reached the top of the mound the horses were where he'd last seen them, making him sigh with relief. Then she slipped out from under his arm and mounted up before riding off without waiting for him.

To his surprise she headed downriver. He dallied to wring water out of his soaked clothing and then followed her.

He wondered if she intended to follow the bodies, but she didn't look at the water, and when she reached the end of the mound she turned inland. Then she took the route they had used to try to evade their pursuers, presumably because this path kept the creek out of sight, and after a hundred yards she stopped and waited for him to join her.

'When we meet Finlay, don't hide or excuse what I did,' she said.

'I won't,' he said. 'We'll tell the truth, but don't take all this on yourself. I had to shoot Griffin in self-defence, just like you had to hit Reinhold.'

'I know, but you didn't have good reason to want him dead.'

Lorimer reckoned there was nothing to be gained by arguing with her as she was clearly too concerned about what had happened to be mollified. He reckoned the same would probably go for him, as the deaths of the Devlin brothers meant he was unlikely to ever know for sure whether they had killed Budd.

They rode on in a sombre mood and Abigail didn't even speak when a house came into view. It wasn't on the path they were taking so he looked at her, but she rode for several minutes before she glanced at it and then swung to the side.

He trotted ahead of her and when they reached the house he dismounted and moved to help her down, but she ignored him and rolled out of the saddle on her own.

She moved towards the house, taking small steps, but then stopped when the door opened and Finlay came outside.

'It's Abigail Harlow, isn't it?' he said.

Her only response was a small nod, so he turned

to Lorimer. His brow furrowed as he clearly struggled to recognize him.

'Howdy, Sheriff O'Toole,' Lorimer said, stepping forward.

'I'm just Finlay now, but how do. . . ?' He trailed off and smiled. 'I never expected to see Jeremiah Hall's son again.'

'I wish the circumstances could have been better. I returned to Clear Creek because I'd heard he'd died, and that was just the start of my problems.'

Finlay gestured at the door. 'You both look as if you've seen some trouble. Come inside and tell me about it.'

Abigail shuffled forward and Lorimer raised an arm to usher her inside, but then a woman came into the doorway.

'Nobody told me you'd married,' Lorimer said.

'We didn't. We have an arrangement.' Finlay glanced at her. 'It wasn't by design.'

The woman stepped forward and smiled at them both.

'Let me introduce myself,' she said. 'I'm Jessica Templeman.'

CHAPTER 12

'Are you Carl's sister?' Lorimer asked as, with a nervous gesture, he felt the bulge in his pocket made by the watch.

'No, I'm his wife,' she said. 'Do you know something about him?'

Lorimer shook his head. 'No. In fact we have more questions than. . . .'

Lorimer trailed off when Abigail sobbed. Finlay and Jessica turned to her and she raised a hand to show she would be fine, but Finlay caught Jessica's eye and then looked at the house.

With her hand held out, Jessica moved forward and took Abigail's arm. Abigail didn't object and with her head lowered she let Jessica escort her inside.

Finlay watched them until Jessica closed the door and then turned to Lorimer.

'What's distressed her?' he asked.

'She's had a tough time recently,' Lorimer said. 'Her husband got lynched. Then we were attacked a few miles down the creek. We defended ourselves and both men ended up face down in the water.'

'That's a better result than you two ending up there, although Abigail seems concerned with the outcome.'

'That's because we came here to talk to you about the dead men. They were the Devlin brothers. They returned to Clear Creek and they were just as much trouble as the first time they were there.'

Lorimer then related the recent events. He covered the lynching quickly before moving on to his theory that the Devlins had killed Budd Ewing and Manford Wigfall, and finishing with their assault on him the previous night.

'I guess I'm not surprised they came back to cause more trouble.' Finlay glanced at the house and then urged Lorimer to move away from it for a short distance. 'But don't blame them for Budd's death, no matter if Abigail wants to believe them responsible. I'm confident Sheriff Roswell investigated that incident thoroughly.'

'At the time Glenn being responsible seemed the most likely reason, but he didn't know the Devlins were back, so I'd like to hear more about them.'

Finlay frowned. 'I don't know anything that might prove what they've done recently.'

'Then tell me about Carl Templeman.'

Unlike Abigail and Benedict, who had been shocked, Finlay reacted with a smile.

'Why do you want to know about him?'

Lorimer considered various responses, but he figured the quicker he faced up to his mistakes the less guilty he would feel. He withdrew the watch from his pocket and held it out.

'This was a gift from Jessica. Manford Wigfall had it on him when he died and I reckon the Devlins might have wanted it.'

Finlay took the watch and nodded when he read the inscription, but then he directed a long look at Lorimer.

'She originally gave it to Carl, but why do you have it?'

'I thought it might be important, so I took it, but I didn't know who to give it to until now.'

Finlay narrowed his eyes and Lorimer reckoned he would accuse him, but then with a shrug he appeared to dismiss the matter.

'I can see no reason why the Devlins would be interested in this watch, but it sure interests me.' Finlay held the watch tightly and gestured at him with it. 'Every lawman has an unsolved investigation that gnaws at them after they've retired. Carl Templeman was mine.'

Lorimer frowned. 'I didn't know he was being investigated.'

'Before you left, he wasn't. Back then the usual

three poker players were your father, Benedict Harlow and Manford Wigfall. There was no regular fourth person and on the night the Devlins stormed the forge they'd invited a man who had just been passing through.'

'So after the shooting Carl moved on?'

Finlay walked a few paces away from him and then returned, his thoughtful expression suggesting he was thinking about what he should tell him.

'At the time, that's what I thought, and as everyone else gave a full account of that night's events I never questioned the matter, but months afterwards his wife sought me out.' He gestured at the house. 'Carl had gone missing and she was looking for him.'

'And his trail led her to Clear Creek?'

Finlay nodded. 'It also went cold there. Jessica had heard the rumour he'd struck lucky at poker, but she didn't know where. I helped her as best I could, but I couldn't find out where he went after leaving here.'

Lorimer looked at the house. Through the window he saw that Jessica was talking while Abigail was holding a blanket around her shoulders and looking more relaxed than she had done earlier.

'She's still here, so I guess she didn't get any answers.'

'Jessica continued searching, and a few years later when I retired I tracked her down. She'd accepted she'd never find him alive, but she still wanted to solve the mystery.' Finlay rubbed the back of his neck while giving a sheepish smile. 'I helped her and we got close, but the mystery remains unsolved.'

Lorimer leaned towards Finlay and smiled.

'You're an ex-lawman. You must have a theory.'

Finlay's eyes flickered and he glanced at the watch, this comment appearing to trouble him.

'I do, and it's the obvious one. After Carl won at poker he came to Clear Creek and got into another game. The Devlins heard he had money and planned to steal it. They failed, so before I arrested them they followed him, jumped him and dumped the body somewhere.'

'It's a fine theory, but they came back to look for him, presumably to get his money, so he couldn't have been killed.'

'That's by no means certain, but it does mean that for the first time in years I have new information. The only question is: where does it lead me?'

Finlay again looked troubled and not like a man who might have taken a big step towards solving an old mystery.

'What aren't you telling me?' Lorimer asked.

Finlay tipped back his hat and sighed before he looked Lorimer in the eye.

'As nobody has seen Carl Templeman in ten years, my other theory makes sense, too.'

Finlay opened his hand to display the watch, making Lorimer frown.

'If the Devlins didn't kill him, someone else did, and Manford having the watch is mighty suspicious.'

Finlay nodded. 'The only people who spent time with him in Clear Creek were the other poker players.'

'But two of those men were shot and. . . .' Lorimer trailed off when he noted that the only player not to have been hurt that night was his father, but he couldn't work out if that made him more or less likely to have been involved in whatever happened to Carl.

'This is only a possibility and someone not even connected to the game could have done it, but on the other hand those men never played poker together again.'

'And afterwards the feuding started.' Lorimer sighed. 'Abigail fears the bad blood started because Budd and Glenn argued over her and her sister. I hate the thought it happened because Budd and me got dragged into the Devlins' scheme. But maybe neither of those is the reason.'

'Maybe.' Finlay rubbed his hands together. 'But we won't get no answers standing here. I'll head back to Clear Creek and speak with Sheriff Roswell.'

'I'd be obliged if you would. The sheriff is mighty suspicious of me and my motives.'

Finlay chuckled, now seemingly more relaxed after revealing the matter he had been reluctant to mention.

'So nothing's changed there.'

Lorimer joined him in laughing. Then they headed to the house.

As Lorimer had observed earlier, Abigail was no longer agitated, although their arrival made Jessica look at Finlay with concern. Finlay took her aside and explained briefly what Lorimer had told him and then he gave her the watch. She fingered it with her head bowed before declaring her intention to accompany them to Clear Creek.

Finlay didn't object, so in short order they left the house and rode downriver, taking the route that Lorimer and Abigail had used. Jessica rode beside Lorimer and asked him to tell her everything he knew about Carl.

Jessica then talked about her search for him. By the time she'd finished they'd reached the scene of the Devlins' demise.

They stopped and Lorimer talked Finlay through the incident. Abigail stayed quiet, the discussion seeming to depress her again.

Finlay accepted his version of events, so when they set off Lorimer hoped they wouldn't face any repercussions. For the first few miles they looked out for the two bodies floating downriver, but as they didn't see them Lorimer's thoughts turned to

Finlay's theories about what had happened to Carl
Templeman.

When they first saw Harlow's Bend ahead it was
an hour before sundown, and Lorimer was no
nearer to deciding whether he thought the Devlins
or one of the poker players had killed Carl.

As it was likely that only Benedict could provide
an answer, he expected that Finlay would accompany them to Benedict's house, but Finlay reported
that he would head into town to speak with Sheriff
Roswell.

Lorimer didn't object, although a few minutes
after they had parted ways he wished he had. Sheriff
Roswell was talking with Benedict outside his house.

The two men stopped talking to watch them
approach. Benedict appeared to notice Abigail's
sombre demeanour as he peered at her anxiously,
while Roswell glared at Lorimer with his arms
folded.

'You ignored my order and left town,' Roswell
said when they drew up.

Lorimer didn't reply until he and Abigail had dismounted.

'I also came back and I returned with a friend,'
he said. 'If you have a problem with my decision, go
back to town and talk to Finlay O'Toole. He went
there to speak to you.'

The mention of the former sheriff made Roswell
raise his eyebrows in surprise and he took a few

moments to reply.

'I guess you told him the same lies you told me, but no matter. I'll pay him the courtesy of talking this through with him.'

Lorimer considered whether he should say nothing more and let Finlay explain what had happened earlier, but he figured that if he kept quiet Roswell might take that to mean he had something to hide.

'I can wait to hear the result of that conversation as the danger has passed. The Devlin brothers are dead. They attacked me and Abigail near Finlay's house and we defended ourselves.'

Roswell snorted. 'That sure is convenient for you.'

Lorimer gave a wry smile. 'I should have expected that response, but Abigail saw everything. The incident troubled her, but when she's calmer she'll talk to you. Please be gentle with her.'

His comment made Benedict move on to stand with Abigail, who murmured that she'd be fine. He still urged her to join him in the house, and she complied without further comment.

'Your compassion for her is touching,' Roswell said as he watched them walk to the door. 'You're probably the only person aside from Benedict that's had a kind word to say about her, and I'm sure that'll—'

'Quit pouring scorn on everything I say and do.

The Devlins attacked me twice and they killed Manford. Before that they probably killed Budd, too.'

Roswell licked his lips and moved closer to him, but he didn't reply immediately as he watched the door until it closed, his eager grin showing he would enjoy making his response.

'They didn't kill Budd, so there's no reason to connect them to the other incidents.'

'What makes you certain about that?'

Roswell set his hands on his hips. 'The Devlins got nine years in jail and that sentence ended around ten months ago.'

Lorimer shrugged. 'So they had plenty of time to stew over their treatment, plan their revenge, and enact it.'

Roswell shook his head. 'Except I've just learnt that they caused a heap of trouble in jail, so their sentences were extended. Two months ago, when Budd was killed, they were still behind bars.'

Lorimer started to smile, but then checked himself when the full ramifications of this revelation hit him.

'So Budd's death had nothing to do with them,' he murmured. 'And Glenn probably killed Budd after all.'

'That matter was decided in court. It's yet to be decided about Manford.' Roswell looked him over. 'Luckily I already have a culprit in mind, so make sure you're still here when I return.'

With that, Roswell headed to his horse and rode off towards town.

CHAPTER 13

Lorimer watched Roswell until he'd disappeared from view. Then he stood for several minutes while rubbing his jaw to try to avoid smiling, but he failed.

Roswell's threat didn't feel as important as the news he had given him. The fact that the Devlins hadn't killed Budd both relieved him and made him feel proud of the decision he'd made the previous night.

He had pursued the truth even though it could have shown he'd let an innocent man die. He had still failed Glenn and there was still a chance he'd been the victim of a miscarriage of justice, but his worst fears had been unfounded.

He moved on to the door and the moment he opened it his good mood ended. Abigail was sitting at the table while Benedict knelt at her side.

They were talking using low voices, but they broke off to look at him. They both had calm expressions suggesting they'd discussed the incident by the creek and it had given them some peace of mind.

Lorimer closed his eyes briefly and took deep breaths, now finding that he wished Roswell hadn't told him about the Devlins as he'd prefer dealing with his own guilt rather than plunging them back into torment. He walked to the table and sat opposite them.

'As you heard, Sheriff Roswell is sceptical about the incident upriver,' he said. 'He'll question you later.'

'He has to believe us!' Abigail spluttered. 'Finlay O'Toole sure did and it's obvious they wanted to kill us.'

'He saw no reason why they'd do that. He didn't see them last night and he didn't see them when they attacked Manford.'

'The man's a fool,' Benedict muttered.

'I don't reckon so.' Lorimer sighed as he struggled to complete his explanation, and his concern must have been obvious as Abigail and Benedict looked at him intently. 'They didn't kill Budd. They were in jail at the time.'

'They didn't. . . .' Benedict trailed off and looked at Abigail, who opened and closed her mouth several times before she found the right words.

'That doesn't mean Glenn did it,' she said.

'It doesn't.' Benedict laid a hand on her arm. 'We

won't rest until we know the truth.'

She looked doubtful and so did Benedict. Then they both looked at Lorimer with concerned expressions as they implored him to provide a suggestion.

Lorimer didn't have an alternative suspect in mind, but he didn't reckon he'd get a better chance to bring up the worrying matter that Finlay had told him.

'We tried to find out who did it and we failed,' he said. 'So perhaps we should look at the reason why Budd was killed, which means working out why there was bad blood between him and Glenn.'

He watched Benedict for his reaction, but it was Abigail who became the most animated. She jumped to her feet and walked to the window.

'You're right,' she said. 'We've avoided that question for too long.'

'What do you suggest we do?' Benedict said, getting to his feet.

For long moments she thought about the matter and then stamped a foot on the floor.

'I suggest I take a walk before it gets dark.'

With that she headed to the door. Benedict watched her with concern, but he didn't try to stop her leaving, and when she'd gone outside he turned to Lorimer.

'After the day she's had, she needs to spend some time alone to think this through.'

Lorimer nodded. 'I hope she comes up with an answer, as I don't know whether the feud was over her and her sister, the raid on the poker game, or something else. But with Finlay involved, we might find out more as he's interested in Carl Templeman, a man he reckons died ten years ago.'

Benedict flinched. His concerned reaction didn't surprise Lorimer, but before he could question him Benedict pointed outside.

'We have to go,' he said. 'Abigail isn't just going for a walk.'

Lorimer reckoned Benedict was trying to avoid an uncomfortable subject, but when he joined him at the window he accepted he was right to be concerned. Abigail was striding across Harlow's Bend towards her sister's house, having clearly decided to no longer wait for Christina to come to see her.

Without further comment the two men hurried outside and headed to their horses. By the time they had mounted up, Abigail had reached the middle of the bend, so he doubted they could intercept her in time to avoid a confrontation, but they still set off at a fast trot.

They had covered a quarter of the way to her when she looked over her shoulder. She shook her head and then gave a dismissive wave before breaking into a run.

A short while later the uneven terrain took her from their view. The two men glanced at each other and frowned as they accepted they would fail to stop her and, sure enough, when they reached the point where she had disappeared from view, Abigail was already confronting Christina.

They were standing in front of the house, with the White brothers looking on from beside the forge. Abigail and Christina didn't appear to notice the approaching riders as they gestured and shouted at each other.

'Budd's dead,' Christina was saying as Lorimer drew his horse to a halt. 'Nothing can change that.'

'Glenn's dead, too, but we're sisters and nothing can change that,' Abigail said.

'What happened that day changed everything. It can never go back to the way it was.'

'I know that, but we have to go forward and there are too many unanswered questions. Neither of us know why it happened and maybe if we talked it through we might get an answer.'

'The answer will always be the same: that Glenn killed Budd, except you still hope it'll be a different one.' Christina gestured, indicating the other side of the bend. 'Go away and don't waste my time again until you accept the truth.'

That demand was the cue for Vester and Moody to move towards Abigail, so Lorimer and Benedict dismounted and hurried on to stand with her.

'She came here in good faith,' Benedict said. 'You have to talk one day. It might as well be today.'

'I don't see no good faith. You come here with guns demanding answers.'

'I'm not. . . .' Benedict trailed off and glanced at Lorimer's gun.

This observation appeared to give the brothers second thoughts about confronting them as Vester stopped while Moody hurried back to the forge. It was likely that when he came out he would be armed, so Lorimer walked towards Christina with his arms spread wide.

'There's no need for trouble,' he said. 'Sheriff Roswell and Finlay O'Toole will be here soon with questions, so we should talk it through before they arrive.'

Christina firmed her jaw looking as if she'd refuse his request, but then with a sigh her shoulders sagged, as she appeared to lose the will to fight.

'Go on, then. Talk, but only you and not those two.'

Christina gestured at Abigail and Benedict, and although they murmured to each other they didn't retort. Moody then came out of the forge armed with a six-shooter, but he kept it lowered.

Lorimer stopped a few paces away from Christina and adopted a casual stance, as if he was about to mention a minor matter.

'From what I've learnt, Glenn may have argued with Budd because he had feelings for you.'

'He didn't,' Christina snapped. 'Those rumours

were just plain wicked.'

She glanced at Abigail, who murmured in relief.

'In that case something else caused the ill-feeling,' Lorimer said. 'Budd's involvement with the Devlins got Benedict shot and that angered Glenn, but now I wonder if the feuding started because of another incident: the mysterious disappearance of Carl Templeman.'

Christina gave a small nod while Moody's gun-arm twitched with a possibly unconscious gesture that confirmed they both thought this matter was important. Vester stood rigidly, his attempt not to show a reaction appearing studied enough to make Lorimer turn to him.

In response, Vester turned away and his gaze lingered on a point near to the creek before he moved off to join his brother. His long look reminded Lorimer of an earlier time when he had looked at the trees.

That thought made Lorimer try to work out where Vester had been looking and he murmured to himself in triumph when he noted he'd again looked at the trees. His father's grave was there, but so was another unmarked grave.

'Glenn argued with Budd about that man,' Christina said. 'I guess it could be the reason why he killed him, but we'll never know now.'

'You're wrong,' Lorimer said. 'Tell Vester to fetch a spade. Then we'll uncover the truth.'

'What use is a spade right now?' Christina spluttered.

By the forge, Moody and Vester whispered to each other. Their secretive behaviour made Abigail step forward to join Lorimer.

With only Benedict not moving, Christina looked at each person in turn with a furrowed brow as she tried to figure out what everyone else thought Lorimer meant. Lorimer gave a thin smile and pointed at the trees.

'We're going to dig up Carl's body,' he said. 'Then we'll wait for Sheriff Roswell to arrive and figure out where that discovery leads us.'

Christina gave an exasperated sigh, suggesting she didn't believe him, but she turned to the forge and beckoned for Vester to comply with his demand. Vester rocked from foot to foot, but then with a slow shake of the head he sloped off inside.

While they waited for him to return, Abigail edged closer to Lorimer.

'I don't know what you're doing,' she said.

Lorimer shrugged. 'To be honest I'm not sure myself, but I resolved to follow the truth no matter where it led me and I reckon Carl's fate explains the problems at Harlow's Bend.'

She frowned, but she didn't reply as Vester then walked out of the forge holding a spade in each hand. He came over to join them and held out one of the spades to Lorimer.

126

'We dig,' he said.

Vester no longer looked as worried as he had done earlier. Lorimer reckoned that meant the brothers had hatched a plan and he needed to be careful, so he gestured for the armed Moody to join them and for Vester to walk ahead of him.

Both brothers complied, albeit slowly. Then, with Lorimer and Moody casting sideways glances at each other, they made their way to the trees.

Abigail and Benedict stayed together as they followed them while Christina trailed along at the back.

Lorimer waited until everyone had arrived. Then, with his back to the creek and the setting sun, to keep the gathering in front of him, he stood beside the final grave in the line of four, the one that had no inscription.

'Who's buried here?' he asked.

For several seconds everyone stayed quiet with nobody looking at him or at the grave. With a shake of the head Christina was the first to speak up.

'It was there when I started living here with Budd,' she said. 'I assumed there was a family connection as it's near to Jeremiah's wife.'

'It wasn't there when I left home,' Lorimer said. 'So whose could it be?'

'I don't know.' Christina sighed. 'Although I reckon you have a theory.'

'I do.' Lorimer raised his spade. 'And now we'll test it.'

127

Vester had a short, whispered conversation with Moody and then stood on the other side of the grave. He looked Lorimer in the eye and smirked before slamming the spade down into the mound of earth.

Lorimer started work on the other side of the mound and, working in unison, they tossed the compacted dirt aside. He kept one eye on the watching group as he tried to gauge their reactions.

Abigail and Christina watched proceedings with interest. They even edged a few paces closer to each other, perhaps from them both sensing they might soon learn something that would help them deal with their troubling situation.

Moody and Vester were relaxed, seemingly having gotten over the shock caused by Lorimer voicing his theory. At first Lorimer reckoned they were feigning a confident air while Moody waited for the right moment to draw a gun on him, but by the time they'd cleared most of the mound, Lorimer wondered whether they didn't reckon Carl was buried here and they had been worried about something else.

The demeanour of the final person intrigued Lorimer the most. Benedict stood with the others, but his haunted look made him appear as if his thoughts were elsewhere.

The sun had set and the light level was dropping when they started digging below ground level.

Lorimer worked more carefully. The extensive tree roots meant the body would be only a few feet down and he didn't want to damage it.

Vester showed no such caution as he slammed the spade down into the ground and tossed earth aside. He soon paid for his reckless behaviour when a savage downward thrust crunched the blade into a solid object.

With a curse and a wringing of his hands, Vester dropped the spade. Lorimer moved in and found that he had unearthed a thick tree root.

Lorimer scraped the dirt away on both sides of the root, revealing that it was even larger than he had at first thought. It was also several feet further down than he had dug, and he had thought he must be getting close to the body.

He stood back and imagined where the root would go under the earth they had yet to clear. He noted the numerous smaller roots coming off the central one and that led him to an unwelcome conclusion.

As the roots would spread out and cover the whole area, the grave couldn't contain a body.

CHAPTER 14

'There's nothing buried under here but roots,' Lorimer said.

He slammed the spade down into the ground and it crunched against another solid object even though he'd picked a spot away from the uncovered root. He repeated the action twice more in different places, with the same result.

'So your theory was wrong,' Christina said, her low tone sounding disappointed.

'It was, but then again perhaps that doesn't matter. The more important point is what did each of us expect to find?'

'I didn't know what to expect.' She glanced at the others and she appeared to pick on their differing reactions as she nodded.

'You didn't, but what about everyone else?' Lorimer asked.

He turned to Benedict, who was standing stiffly

and showing no interest in proceedings, but Christina faced her cousins.

'You two behaved as if you knew we'd find nothing,' she said.

Vester and Moody turned to her, their contented expressions disappearing in a moment.

'Why are you accusing us?' Moody said. 'We were just helping Lorimer make a fool of himself.'

'I saw that. You were eager to get this done, but why would you know that was an empty grave?'

For long moments silence reigned. Even when the obvious answer came to Lorimer he said nothing as he waited to see how they'd react now that, for the first time, Christina had stopped presenting a united front with them.

'Because they'd dug it up already,' Abigail said, breaking the silence.

'Is that true?' Christina said. 'Have you opened that grave before? Did you find out who was buried there? Was it Carl Templeman?'

Moody had been shaking his head during Christina's questions, but after the final one he turned to Benedict.

'Why don't you ask him?' he said. 'We weren't even here when Carl came to town and he knows more than we do.'

Everyone turned to Benedict, who took several moments before he registered he was being spoken about. With a faltering gait he moved to the hole and peered into it.

The light level was dropping with every passing moment and the low moonlight didn't illuminate the bottom of the hole, so he moved around seeking a better angle. Then he gathered up Vester's dropped spade and shovelled earth away.

Nobody tried to stop him and after a minute of steady work his shoulders slumped over and he murmured something to himself. Then he swirled round to face Vester and hurled the spade at him with a roar of anger.

'When did you do this?' he shouted as Vester ducked away and avoided the spinning spade. 'How did you. . . ?'

He didn't get to complete his question as Moody raised his gun and blasted lead at him. As Benedict dropped to his knees while murmuring in pain, Lorimer aimed his gun at Moody, but Moody showed no sign of firing again as Christina advanced on him, her firm gait suggesting she would remonstrate with him.

Even Vester looked at Moody with surprise, so with it looking as if the confrontation wouldn't escalate, Abigail hurried to the wounded man and Lorimer joined her.

Abigail reached Benedict first and knelt beside him. She placed a hand on his back, but her gentle action made Benedict twitch and topple over on to his side.

'Where's he been shot?' Lorimer asked.

She shrugged, but then Benedict curled up and clutched his upper chest, identifying the location of the wound. Acting quickly, Lorimer got him to lie on his back while Abigail ripped off a length of cloth from the bottom of her skirt to cover the wound.

She appeared to have a better idea about how to look after him than Lorimer had, so he backed away to give her room to work and then glanced up to see what the others were doing. Moody was striding back towards the forge while Vester ushered Christina along after him.

Abigail followed Lorimer's gaze and then winced.

'I can look after him,' she said. 'Help her.'

'Your cousins won't harm her.'

'I'm not so sure. She questioned their behaviour. They didn't like that.'

Lorimer looked again at the retreating group and this time he noticed that Vester was shoving Christina along with so much force she stumbled after every push. As they followed Moody through the doorway she looked back at them with concern, which made Vester push her again.

Lorimer nodded to Abigail and set off, but as he passed her, Benedict thrust out a hand and grabbed his leg.

'We never meant for it to happen,' he said, his voice weak.

Abigail patted his shoulder and then pressed the wadded cloth tightly against his wound.

'We don't need to hear this now,' she said. 'Rest.'

'I might not have the time.' He looked at Lorimer, who went to one knee beside him. 'We invited Carl to join the game when we heard he'd won big. We planned a ruse to fleece him, but it didn't work.'

'I'd already gathered the last part. The Devlins heard about his big win and raided before the game got going.'

Benedict shook his head. 'They did, but that's not the worst part. It was all in vain. . . .'

Benedict trailed off, his eyes becoming unfocussed. Then he coughed and the action made a spasm of pain contort his body.

Lorimer and Abigail lay soothing hands on him until he settled back down. Abigail then met Lorimer's eye and shook her head.

'He doesn't need to concern himself with this. Help Christina and then later we'll piece together what happened.'

Lorimer nodded, and after directing a comforting smile at Benedict he got up and headed towards the forge. He was moving past the last tree when Moody poked his head out through the doorway.

Moody glared at him and then slipped his gun into view. His expression was so angry it made Lorimer throw himself to the ground and lie on his front.

Moody still fired. Lorimer didn't see where the gunshot landed, but he figured that as he was lying in a patch of darkened ground Moody wouldn't be able to see him clearly.

He shuffled a few feet to the side and then thrust his gun out in front of him. He steadied his aim and fired at Moody.

The shot clattered into the wall a foot above Moody's head causing him to jerk back out of sight. Lorimer adjusted his aim and waited, but when several minutes passed without Moody appearing again, he got to his feet and broke into a run.

With his gun trained on the doorway he headed for the side of the forge nearest the creek, and he reached the corner of the building without mishap. He gathered his breath and then made his way along the side wall to the far corner where he stood a few feet from the back entrance.

Inside Christina was speaking and although he couldn't hear her words her tone sounded aggrieved. He edged closer to the door and, thankfully, Christina raised her voice.

'Where did you take the body?' she demanded.

'That's not important,' Vester said from nearby. 'Glenn and Budd argued about Carl, so they must have suspected something.'

Christina muttered under her breath and footfalls sounded as she moved across the forge towards

Vester. Then Moody spoke up from the front doorway.

'We did it for all of us,' he said. 'After the trouble here Jeremiah Hall's business never recovered, what with him and Benedict arguing and his drinking. More trouble would have destroyed our business.'

'What you did kept the arguments going, and Budd's death won't make people think the forge is a safe place to use, will it?'

'I know you don't want anyone speaking ill of your husband, but he should have let the matter drop.'

Christina gasped and when she spoke again her voice was lower.

'Are you saying Budd talked about Carl's body with you, too?'

Neither man replied. As long moments passed in silence, Lorimer could imagine the three people glaring at each other, a long-delayed argument having reached a crucial moment.

He hadn't heard all of the discussion, but clearly the relationship between Christina and her protective cousins wasn't as friendly as he had thought. It was also clear that the brothers had secrets of their own and that led Lorimer to a shocking conclusion.

When Vester and Moody killed Glenn he had assumed it was an act of revenge, but another motive made just as much sense: dealing with a loose thread to bury the truth that they had killed Budd.

Christina's questions suggested she'd reached the same conclusion.

He stepped forward to look into the forge and he had been broadly right about everyone's positions. Vester had his back to him, while Moody had turned away from the doorway to join his brother in facing Christina, who was standing beside the firebox.

'We told Budd that Jeremiah talked about some of the events after the poker game,' Vester said at last with a glance at Moody. 'That wasn't enough for Budd. He wanted to know what we did with the body and he wouldn't let the matter drop. He got all riled up and later that day he met Glenn. The rest you know.'

'I know that the day ended with Budd dead and Glenn claiming he saw two men riding away from the scene.'

'Glenn lied.'

'Did he?' She waited and when neither man replied she raised her voice. 'Did he? Did he?'

She looked from one man to the other and back again, her movements becoming more agitated, but then she noticed Lorimer and she stopped moving. A thin smile appeared and that got the brothers' attention, with Vester standing up straight and Moody turning to him.

Lorimer snapped up his gun arm and at the same

moment Moody raised his own gun. Neither man fired, so they ended up with Lorimer aiming at Vester's back and Moody aiming at him.

'Answer her question,' Lorimer said as he took steady paces into the forge.

Neither of the brothers replied, and when he drew level with Vester he held out a hand to Abigail, who set off towards him, but that made Vester turn to him.

'She's not going nowhere with you,' he said.

'This is over,' Lorimer said. 'Soon everyone will know what you did to Budd and then to Glenn. Your only hope is to get as far away from here as you can.'

'Except we know what happened to Carl, and then there's the full story of Glenn's death. Do you want us to reveal all that?'

'Do it. The truth should come out.'

Lorimer must have spoken with conviction as Vester snarled and advanced on him. Lorimer backed away while shaking his head with a warning, but Vester took another pace and then leapt at him.

Seeing no choice, Lorimer fired, his shot slicing into Vester's chest and making him slam down to the floor at his feet. Lorimer then twisted aside while turning to Moody, but his other opponent didn't fire as Christina had moved between them.

She was staring at Vester in shock so her action hadn't been by design, but Lorimer took advantage and leapt to the floor. Then he scrambled along on hands and knees, aiming to use the firebox as cover.

He stopped five feet from the box and, on his knees, faced the doorway while gesturing at Christina to run to the other exit. The wounded Vester was still holding her attention and she didn't move, so he raised his head and looked for Moody.

He could see most of the doorway where Moody had been standing the last time he'd seen him, so he presumed he'd headed for cover, too. He ducked down and shuffled closer to the firebox.

The box was radiating heat so he avoided touching it. Keeping his head below the top of the side panel he looked to either side.

The only movement came from Christina going to one knee beside Vester and looking him over. She frowned and turned to the firebox.

Lorimer thought she was interested in him until he noticed she was looking above him. Her behaviour puzzled him, but then a crunch sounded.

He turned while looking up and it was to find that Moody had approached him from the only direction he hadn't expected. He had vaulted into the firebox, braving the smouldering embers, and he was now looming up over him.

Moody was aiming his gun down at a point a few feet to Lorimer's side, having presumably not known his exact location, so Lorimer scrambled away in the other direction. From the corner of his eye he saw Moody adjust his aim, but by then he had reached the corner of the box.

As Moody fired, he threw himself to the floor at the back of the box and drew his legs up. His face was only inches from the back panel and the heat made him flinch away.

He accepted that Moody was more resilient to the heat than he was, but he didn't reckon he could stand in the embers indefinitely. He raised his gun to shoulder height and leapt up.

He aimed his gun towards the middle of the box, and his assumption that Moody wouldn't be able to withstand the heat for much longer proved correct as his opponent was already leaping forward. Moody ploughed into him.

Lorimer fell back and both men went down. Moody's weight slammed down on Lorimer's chest and blasted the air from his lungs.

While Lorimer coughed and floundered, Moody raised himself off him and grabbed his arm. Then he dragged him to his feet and launched him towards the firebox.

Lorimer stumbled along for three paces and then slammed against the back panel. He tipped over and went crashing down on to his side amidst the embers.

Frantically he rolled and came up on his feet. To

his surprise he felt no pain, but he was facing Moody, who smirked at him, the smoke rising from his boots shrouding his form.

Moody raised his gun arm, and as the first spots of heat rippled across his soles Lorimer registered that he'd kept hold of his gun. He snapped up his gun arm and fired, acting on instinct and not having time to aim.

Moody froze with his gun not yet aimed at him. Then a red bloom spread out from his forehead and he toppled over backwards.

Lorimer enjoyed a moment of relief, but then the heat intensified and with a squeal of pain he bounded to the side and leapt out of the box. He danced from side to side, kicking at the floor and scuffing his feet until he settled for dropping down on his rump and raising his feet off the floor.

His boots were smoking, but with his weight no longer pressing his soles against them the heat lessened rapidly. Now confident of avoiding harm he looked at Christina, who had broken off from trying to help Vester to look at Moody.

She shook her head and then turned to Lorimer.

'They gave you no choice,' she said.

'They didn't, but I still wish things could have been different,' he said.

'Maybe, but you said they'd done something to Budd and Glenn. Does that mean what I reckon it means?'

141

Lorimer nodded. When she lowered her head, he got to his feet and scuffed his feet along the floor again.

By the time he'd confirmed that his boots were no longer burning, she had returned to fussing over Vester. Lorimer presumed she wanted him to survive so he could face justice and she could get the full story, but without further comment he headed to the door.

Outside, Abigail and Benedict weren't visible in the gloom, so fearing the worst he walked towards the trees slowly. The thought then came that during the chaos in the forge he hadn't considered the fact that if the brothers had killed Budd, he now knew for certain that he had stood by and let an innocent man be killed.

He bowed his head and trudged along. When he reached the first tree he stopped and peered at the spot where Benedict had been lying the last time he had seen him.

He wasn't there, so he looked towards Benedict's house, presuming that Abigail was helping him get back home. As he still failed to see either person, he moved on and he had reached the next tree when a footfall sounded to his side.

With a smile on his lips he turned, but the smile died when a man came out from behind the tree holding Abigail at gunpoint. He feared that the wounded Benedict had taken leave of his senses, but then the man moved into a patch of moonlight, revealing his features.

The assailant was Reinhold Devlin.

CHAPTER 15

'I thought you'd drowned,' Lorimer said, lost for anything else to say.

'I nearly did, thanks to you two,' Reinhold said. He stepped back behind the tree leaving Abigail still visible. 'I floated downriver for hours before I could scramble back to the side, and I couldn't find my brother.'

Abigail tensed up, suggesting Reinhold hadn't questioned her about Griffin's fate.

'I'm sure he'll wash up safe and sound somewhere.'

'You shot him. He'll need help and if he doesn't get it, I'll make what happened here ten years ago seem like a picnic.'

'Then we'd better get a search underway. It won't be easy in the dark.'

'It won't, so while you find him I'll look after her. Fail and she dies.' Reinhold came back into view briefly and looked towards the final grave in the line. 'I reckon Benedict might not survive whether you succeed or not, so hurry.'

His comment made Abigail murmur under her breath. Fearing that Reinhold was right, Lorimer raised his hands to shoulder height and took a step to the side so his opponent could see him, although Reinhold was still shrouded in shadows.

'Let her and Benedict go,' he said. 'It's me you have a problem with.'

'I sure do and your only chance of living is to—'

'Don't waste your breath on that threat. Just shoot me and let the others go.' Lorimer took another pace to the side, letting him see more of Reinhold's form, and in a sign that she knew what he intended to say Abigail shook her head. 'Griffin is dead.'

'How do you know that?' Reinhold muttered.

'I don't, but he got shot and he floated away face down in the water.'

'I reckon I must have done that as well, as when I came to I coughed up so much water I'm surprised there's any left in the creek. He doesn't have to be dead. He doesn't!'

Reinhold glared at Lorimer, his wide eyes demanding that he agree with him. Lorimer only shook his head and with a snarl of anguish Reinhold shoved Abigail away from him.

She stumbled and went down on her knees. Then

she began crawling towards the endmost grave where, presumably, Benedict was lying.

Lorimer watched her until she moved behind the next tree and then faced Reinhold. He spread his hands.

'Go on. Do it. I'm sure that finding Carl Templeman's money no longer matters to you.'

Reinhold snorted. 'So you believe that nonsense, do you?'

'It's not nonsense. I've learnt most of the story about him since we last met, and Moody and Vester filled in the missing pieces.'

'Except nobody told you that Carl never had no money.' Reinhold looked triumphantly at Lorimer, his grin growing when he didn't reply. 'Carl was working with us. He convinced those fools he'd won big so they'd bring heaps of money to the game.'

'And then you'd steal it?'

'No. He had a few tricks up his sleeve as well as a few cards, and he reckoned he could win at the table. Then we'd help him make a quick exit, but they must have worked out the truth as they attacked him. We only went in the forge to help him.'

Lorimer hadn't seen enough of the events of that night to know if this was true. He shrugged.

'No matter what your intentions were, two Clear Creek men got shot that night.'

'And no matter who you believe, we now know

that later that night Carl was killed. So who do you believe?'

'I believe the court. They heard the—'

'We never got no proper justice,' Reinhold snapped. 'Everyone had already made up their minds about us and if we'd have talked nobody would have listened to our story.'

Reinhold glared at Lorimer, defying him to argue with his version of events. When he didn't reply he gestured with his gun for Lorimer to turn around.

Lorimer did as he'd been told and Reinhold disarmed him. Then a shove to the back made him walk to the other side of the trees and along to the grave where Carl had once been buried.

Abigail was kneeling beside Benedict, who was lying quietly holding the wadded and bloodied cloth to his chest. She looked at Lorimer with an aggrieved expression, her demeanour showing she had heard Reinhold's accusation.

'Don't believe his lies,' she said. 'Benedict is a good man.'

'I don't,' Lorimer said. 'Reinhold and Griffin were troublemakers.'

Reinhold stepped up closer to Lorimer and shoved him forward.

'Not always and not as bad as some,' Reinhold said and then raised his voice. 'Benedict, tell them everything you did that night. Then we can all finally know the truth and I can kill Lorimer.'

Benedict only murmured to himself, seemingly in too much pain to talk. Reinhold snorted and shoved Lorimer again.

Lorimer tried to stand his ground, but he still took a half-pace forward and that made his ankle brush against the handle of the spade Vester had used earlier. It was lying in a pool of darkness so he doubted that Reinhold had noticed it.

He stepped back and that made Reinhold shove him more firmly. This time Lorimer stumbled deliberately.

He went to one knee and slapped a hand on the handle. He steadied himself and then rose up while twisting round towards Reinhold.

With the force of his quick movement behind it, the spade swung round towards his opponent's chest. At the last moment Reinhold ducked and the blade went slicing through the air above his lowered shoulders.

Lorimer stopped the spade and swung it back towards Reinhold, who raised his gun arm as he prepared to shoot. A moment before he fired the flat of the blade crunched into his upper arm, jerking the gun to the side, and the shot flew several feet wide of Lorimer.

Lorimer drew the spade back and batted it against Reinhold's arm a second time. This time the blow sent the gun spinning from his opponent's hand while knocking Reinhold on to his side.

With a yell of triumph, Lorimer advanced on Reinhold and raised the spade above his head as he prepared to dash it down on his supine form, but in desperation Reinhold kicked out. His foot slammed into Lorimer's calf, rocking his body and veering his aim.

The blade sliced into the ground beside Reinhold's chest, and his opponent wasted no time in grabbing the handle. Then the two men strained to gain sole possession of the spade, but Reinhold yanked harder and dragged it towards him until he was holding it sideways above his head.

With a grunt of effort, Lorimer resisted and stopped the handle from moving before he pressed down. The spade went lower with the handle getting closer to Reinhold's throat, but Reinhold locked his elbows, braced himself, and then shoved up and back with a firm motion that made Lorimer topple forward.

Unable to stop himself, he ended up doing a somersault before landing on his back. His grip of the spade came free and he slid down the slope towards the creek for several feet.

He shook himself and turned back towards Reinhold only to find that his opponent was advancing on him and he had raised the spade to shoulder height as he aimed to turn the tables on him. Reinhold stalked around him warily, presumably as he tried to make sure Lorimer didn't try the same tactic on him that he had used.

Then he stabbed the spade down towards Lorimer's chest. Lorimer rolled away from it, but Reinhold's move had been only a feint and even as Lorimer came to a halt on his back he was aiming a second blow at his throat.

With only a moment to react, Lorimer thrust up his arms and grabbed the blade in his left hand and the handle in his right. The spade still moved downwards and Lorimer gritted his teeth, but then exhaled a sigh of relief when he stopped the blade in front of his chin.

Reinhold grunted in irritation and pressed down. Figuring he couldn't hold him off for long, Lorimer twisted aside while releasing the spade, letting it slice into the ground beside his head.

Lorimer rose up quickly while turning to Reinhold, who struggled to move the spade after it had buried itself in a soft patch of ground. Reinhold yanked again and the blade came free, but Lorimer ignored the spade and hammered a round-armed punch into Reinhold's cheek that sent him spinning.

Reinhold lost his hold of the handle, and before the spade could clatter to the ground Lorimer swooped in and gathered it up. Then, while still moving forward, he swung the spade at Reinhold's back.

Reinhold twisted round to face him while

ducking down, but that had the unfortunate result of moving him into the path of the blade, which sliced into the side of his head with a sickening crunch. Reinhold went down, his movement so sudden it tore the handle from Lorimer's grasp.

Lorimer moved to reclaim the spade, but then jerked his hand back when with a gulp he saw that the blade had buried itself in Reinhold's skull. Slowly, the spade toppled over to lie on the ground, but the blade didn't come free, so Lorimer didn't bother checking on his opponent and stepped away from him.

He headed back up the slope to the grave, where Abigail was watching him approach with blank eyes.

'It's over now,' he said. 'He's dead.'

Abigail nodded, her eyes gleaming in the moonlight.

'So is Benedict,' she said.

Lorimer sighed, irritated that the truth about Carl's demise had probably died with him. He looked past her and located Benedict's body lying propped up against a tree.

'Don't think ill of him because of what's been claimed tonight.'

'I don't, but we both saw his reaction, and he said some things before he died.'

She gulped and lowered her head, and when long moments had passed without her explaining further he placed a hand on her arm.

'What did he say?'

'He was so angry about what happened at the poker table that he killed Carl and buried him in a shallow grave a mile downriver.' She looked up at him. 'Manford and Jeremiah kept his secret, but your father felt guilty about his involvement. Some months later he found the body and gave it a proper burial on his land.'

Lorimer nodded. 'And afterwards they could never be friends again, and that led to Budd and Glenn falling out and the White brothers finding out about—'

'That's what happens when you try to hide the truth. At first it works and you reckon you've avoided problems, but then, maybe years later, the past rises up to haunt you and someone pays the price.'

Her comment made Lorimer frown. He released her arm and moved on to stand beside Benedict's body.

He noted that Christina was coming out of the forge, perhaps confirming that Vester had died. Then she stopped and rocked from foot to foot, as she appeared to consider whether to talk with her sister.

There was also movement nearer to town, and when Lorimer narrowed his eyes he discerned that several riders were approaching, presumably in response to the shooting.

As it was likely that Sheriff Roswell would be amongst their number, soon explanations and debate about the evening's events would prevail. He hoped the revelations would be enough to convince the sheriff he hadn't acted improperly recently, but Abigail's words gnawed at him.

He walked back and stood in front of her.

'Can you truly say you're happier knowing that it was Benedict who set off the series of events that led to the recent tragedies?'

'Right now, I can't,' she said with a sigh. 'But later I reckon I'll feel better knowing the truth, and it's likely that me and Christina will find common ground.'

She gestured towards the forge where Christina was making her slow way towards them while glancing at the approaching riders.

Lorimer watched her until she joined them. Then he took a deep breath and looked Abigail in the eye.

'In that case, I have something to tell you,' he said.

Then in clipped tones he gave a matter-of-fact description of the events at Webster's Crossing, leaving nothing out and making no excuses for his behaviour. Christina murmured in disgust when he detailed her cousins' cruel behaviour while Abigail just stared at him with wide eyes.

'You got Glenn killed!' she spluttered when

Lorimer had finished.

'I did,' he said. 'I was stupid, not malicious, and I thought he wouldn't come to harm, but that doesn't change the fact it was my duty to look after him and I failed.'

'I don't know what to say.'

She looked at Christina to speak, but Christina only pointed at the riders. They were now close enough for Lorimer to see that Finlay O'Toole and Jessica Templeman were coming with Sheriff Roswell and Wheeler Ewing.

'Don't say anything,' she said. 'This matter is out of our hands now.'

CHAPTER 16

Lorimer got up at first light and headed to the line of trees where he sat for an hour waiting for the sun to rise.

Christina had let him spend the night in the forge where he had curled up beside the warm firebox. He took that as a sign that she no longer had a problem with him, but he couldn't say the same about Abigail.

She hadn't spoken to him again after Sheriff Roswell had arrived, and long before everyone had finished talking she had returned to Benedict's house.

Roswell had been more reasonable than he had any right to expect, accepting that he had heard the truth at last.

Lorimer had exercised poor judgement, the sheriff had concluded, but he wouldn't face any criminal charges. Lorimer presumed that his conciliatory attitude had resulted from his discussion with Finlay.

When he'd heard the truth about his brother's demise, Wheeler had sloped off back to town in a reflective mood, leaving Finlay and Jessica to try to make sense of the earlier events of the evening. Confirmation of her husband's fate had relieved her while Finlay had nodded approvingly as the missing pieces of the unsolved mystery fitted into place.

'You look thoughtful,' Christina called from behind him, breaking him out of his reverie.

He got up and turned. Christina was no longer wearing black and to his surprise Abigail was with her.

'I wanted to enjoy this spot for one last time,' he said.

'You don't have to move on.'

'I have no reason to stay.'

'You could say the same about us.' Christina gestured at Abigail. 'We've both lost plenty here, but she came to see me late last night and we had a good talk.'

Christina gave Abigail a long look and Lorimer reckoned they'd agreed she'd say something to him. Either way, a minute passed before Abigail coughed and took a step forward.

'I don't blame Christina for what happened to

Glenn and I . . . I don't blame you.'

Lorimer noted her hesitation and he didn't blame her.

'It's all right to be angry with me. I'm angry with me.' He gestured around taking in the whole of Harlow's Bend. 'What are you going to do here now?'

'As neither of us cares what happens to the forge, Christina will come and live with me.'

She pursed her lips as if she wanted to say more, but then she shook her head and headed back to the house. Christina watched her go and then turned to Lorimer.

'She really doesn't blame you. Everything that's gone wrong here happened because ten years ago three men hatched a plan to cheat at poker.'

'It's true that they set off a train of events, but if other people had done the right thing and spoken up that train could have been stopped at any time.'

'I agree, and that's why I'm going to live with Abigail, and why you're welcome to stay on here.'

'I can't.'

Christina edged closer to him, her voice rising.

'Then at least stay for Glenn's funeral; Sheriff Roswell told us that with his investigation over he can be buried tomorrow.'

Lorimer shook his head. 'Abigail won't want me there.'

'She doesn't, but perhaps you need to be around.'

He frowned while searching for the right words to refuse without sounding churlish, but having said her piece Christina didn't give him the time to answer. She turned and headed away.

He watched her until she'd followed Abigail into the house. Then he walked back into the forge and rolled up his blanket.

With the roll tucked under an arm he turned on the spot as he committed to memory what would be his last sight of the place where he'd grown up. He took in the corner where the ill-fated poker game had taken place and finished facing the anvil where he'd so often tried, and failed, to show his father that he could one day become a blacksmith.

He accepted he'd been younger and less strong back then, so on a whim he walked over to the branding iron that Reinhold had nearly used on him. He noted that the upper bar of the T had been poorly aligned, the work not being up to his father's standard.

For some reason that irritated him, so he located a hammer and took the brand to the anvil. A few sharp taps failed to change its shape, so he dropped the blanket and gave it a few stronger taps.

Again the metal resisted his efforts, so he thought back to how his father would have worked the metal. Then he took the brand to the firebox and stoked up the embers.

When the first flames appeared and the heat warmed his hands he thrust the brand in the fire. He waited for a while and this time, when he took it to the anvil, he was able to work the metal.

His ministrations realigned the upper bar of the T and when he admired his work he recalled that Reinhold had reckoned the letter could stand for Templeman. Outside was Templeman's grave, and it was only there because his father had done the right thing and given him a proper burial even though it risked exposing what had happened.

That grave no longer contained Templeman's body and it was likely his final resting place would never be discovered, but he reckoned it was wrong that the man didn't have an inscription to mark his passing.

He rubbed his jaw as he wondered how he could make the other letters to spell out his name in iron. He figured he should start with the easiest letter, which was the L.

That led to the thought that an L could be used twice in another name. He smiled and, with a decision made, he gathered up more wood for the fire.

He took off his jacket, which he hung on the hook on the wall that he hadn't used for ten years.

As the early morning sun shone through the doorway he got to work.

He was still there at sundown.